THE
IMMIGRANT'S
REFRIGERATOR

THE IMMIGRANT'S REFRIGERATOR

STORIES

ELENA GEORGIOU

GENPOP BOOKS

VERMONT 2018

The Immigrant's Refrigerator
© 2018 Elena Georgiou

First edition, February 2018
ISBN-13: 978-0-9985126-4-8
Printed and bound in the USA.

for
the displaced people who are in my family

& for
the 65.3 million displaced people around the world

CONTENTS

All sorrows are less with bread.
—Miguel de Cervantes Saavedra

There is always something left to love.
—Gabriel García Márquez

GAZPACHO

Most days of the week, I stand outside of the train station with two large plastic buckets of gazpacho. Nothing fancy. Mostly mashed up watermelon, onion, cilantro, lime. More to quench their thirsts than to fill their stomachs. The boys come out from their corners. They are quiet. Like their bodies, their movements are small. In their eyes, I see the eyes of my own son. When they realize I have food, they simply say, "Please, Señor?" They don't need to ask. They're the reason I live in this border town. I am here to feed them for the last time before they cross into the U.S. Or for the first time they cross back into Mexico. In either direction, I know their journeys have been long. I want to feed them. I need to feed them. If I don't, who will?

My heart? Oh, my father broke it a long time ago. Because of this, when I feel another crack inside my chest, it frightens me. As god is my witness, I don't know how much heart I have left. Both my own history and these train boys are slowly grinding what is broken inside me into a dust. So. I make soup. I cannot sleep when I think that the only thing these children will take into their bodies are the half-finished cigarettes that others toss away.

3

Fourteen, thirteen, twelve. Friends, brothers. Sometimes, not often, a girl. They are each other's train family—road cousins. They hide on top of *La Bestia*. It is illegal, yes, but there is not much the authorities can do. How can they stop these traveling children when there are hundreds of them riding *el tren de la muerte* each week?

I was once one of them. I made it to the U.S. Two times. Both times, I was sent back. After months in the Migrant Children Detention center, I was happy to be returned to my mother. It didn't matter how good they were to me. It didn't matter how good I was at my lessons. I still felt locked up. Like they were keeping me in a prison. The first time I thought: I did it! I made it! But that America was not like the one on television. TV America is everywhere New York.

After the first time, I thought I would never ride *la bestia* again. But I had to. For my mother. To build her a house with her own bedroom. So she could stop selling food on the street. I wanted to put money in her hands and say, "This is yours. No more cutting your own hair."

I thought that finding my father in America would be the answer to everything. My plan was simple: I would tell him exactly where and how my mother and I had been living, and he would help. Side-by-side, my father and I would work. Side-by-side, we would sign our names at the end of our letters home. Father and son—we would send her our love. And our money.

At the end of my second journey on *la bestia*, I found my father. A miracle!

He said: "It takes more than one night with your mother to make you my son."

He turned his back to me. He closed his door. And all the walls of my life, already built on crumbling foundations, would have fallen on top of me if I hadn't stepped sideways—out of this old house, into the new.

My mother died one year ago—five years after my last border crossing. But I am still building a house for her in my head. I have counted the windows. Seventeen! Also, all the rooms will be on the ground—no stairs—because I want this house to wrap around everyone who enters.

The first time I went on The Beast, I was lucky—I was part of a group, four boys and me. They protected me. We each took it in turns to stay awake and watch out for the others. All five of us had been witnesses to the solo riders. We'd seen how many of them rolled close to the edge of the train while they were dreaming.

When someone rolled off, the train stopped for a moment.

My oldest Road Cousin saw someone roll under the train. He didn't tell us what he saw—how the Dreaming Boy's body was cut, how his legs landed a few feet away from his hands—until the biggest part of our train journey was over and we were close to the U.S. border—the border in all of our dreams.

We all thought that when we got to America we would be adopted by new families, born again into the life we were meant for. Of course we thought we were meant for it; we were just the same as the New York boys on TV. Except their houses had kitchens as big as churches. And refrigerators with so much food, sometimes things were piled on top of each other—with a special place for eggs and cheese and meat.

But now, here I am: a twenty-year-old father who feeds these Road Cousins gazpacho when the train stops to catch its breath in the station. The rest of the day, I drive a hearse. This is my job for money. When I am driving, hardly a day passes when I do not have to "repatriate" a child's body. This is what the authorities tell me to call it when they give me a dead Train Child to take back to his mother. There are so many days I've had to "repatriate" a child's body, it would be easy to lose count.

I have not lost count.

I have repatriated 257 children's bodies.

Each time I load a small coffin into my hearse, a small country turns to dust inside me.

I have a wife now. She came into my life with a child—my stepson. I love him like he is my own. I make sure to hold my boy every day. I don't want him to take *el tren de la muerte*.

"I can't imagine," my wife says, as she stands in the river washing our clothes. I'm smoking my first cigarette of the day, before I have to drive a dead boy back to his mother. "I can't imagine," she says again, "how heavy it must be to carry the death of your child."

It does not matter how many times my wife says *imagine*. I do not imagine. I make gazpacho. When the train's engine comes to a stop, the Cousins jump down from its roof, and I step out with my two buckets. Their hunger rids them of their fear of being out in the open. They form a line. I ladle my soup into their plastic cups.

The Immigrant's Refrigerator

I had the phone in one hand and my door keys in the other when Nicky's Ma forced out some words—*bomb blast, dead.* The information was dry. Our words to each other were dry. But once I'd hung up, my knees gave way and I cried, right there, on the floor, next to the fridge. What stays in my mind all these years is how we expected to die young, for death to come in the shape of a bomb attack or wayward gunfire. We all expected death from the hands of the IRA or the RUC or the UDA or the UVF. Freedom fighters or government troops, Unionists or Loyalists, it didn't matter. It all boiled down to one question: would we be walking in the wrong place at the wrong time? So even though I was half-prepared for the unexpected to be expected, I was still surprised to find my keys in the fridge two days later, on the top shelf between the butter and jam.

Life is not a series of pieces that slot tidily into place. Our lives are often blown apart, the shards flung wide. Then we walk around collecting the fragments, unconvinced that the day will come when we will find all of the missing parts to glue together to form the whole story.

It's been decades since Nicky's death and I have not mislaid a set of keys since. I am in a place in my life where I can call myself happy. I told Plavko this. "You're not happy," he said. "You are living between miseries."

Oh lover, I thought, how wrong you are. I *am* happy. I have love. I have my work. Isn't that all we are supposed to need? I don't really know; Plavko could be right. My default mode is to oversimplify. Love? Work? Is that it? What about disasters—hurricanes? Earthquakes? Floods? Countries bombed? So, yes, I have Love and Work, but maybe I *am* living between miseries? Or maybe—and this feels more likely—there is only one Grand Misery—a backdrop from which happiness occasionally steps forward and gives us a little song and dance.

Plavko is from the Former Yugoslavia. I try to imagine someone asking me where I'm from and having to say, the Former Northern Ireland. It's not so strange. There's the Former Rhodesia, the Former Ceylon, etc. I've made it my business to memorize a list of used-to-be-countries, and if pushed, I can reel off a significant number. Not all—the list keeps changing.

The shards of my life don't fit easily together. But then, nothing about living is easy. Life is not some daytime talkshow where a guest comes on, tells a horrific story, and then tells the audience that he now realizes the only way to free himself is to forgive the person who did those horrible things to him. No, this is the story where the person goes on that show, tells the horrific story, then tells the audience about his realization that the only way to free himself is to forgive the person who did those horrible things to him, and then everyone in the audience is given a washer/dryer and a year's worth of fabric softener—which makes the audience piss their pants with joy—and then The Survivor leaves the TV studio, and as he is hailing a cab—*bam!*—falls down dead from a brain aneurysm.

In this handful of shards, my story begins in the early 90s in Downtown Manhattan. I had recently moved to New York to be a full-time student in a Master of Fine Arts degree program. I wanted to write a collection of short stories. I knew that the idea of paying for an education in short story writing was ridiculous. (If Frank O'Connor didn't need an MFA in writing stories, then I didn't need one, either.) I wasn't enrolled in the program for the education; I was in it because it was a way out of Northern Ireland and because New York City offered me a place where I could be as invisible as I wanted to be. I'd done a wee bit of escort work back home and I knew that this was something I could parlay into keeping my fridge stocked and enough underwear to get me through two weeks without going to the laundromat. Plus, in NYC, I didn't have to worry about my worlds clashing, as they sometimes had in Belfast.

I signed up with a gay escort agency because I wanted to have sex exclusively with men. With gay men, the client base was stable. Plus, they didn't haggle over money when they were paying for sex. I'd done some stripping in my past and it appalled me how little money women were prepared to stuff into my thong. Even when they lost control they never *really* lost control; they always knew *exactly* how much money they were taking out of their purses. The men, well, they knocked back the booze and the money would fly out of their wallets and into my thong in clusters. Fistfuls of paper money stuffed into my underwear made it worth the effort. I didn't mind sweating my arse off to *You make me feel so mighty real*, if I was well paid. But the straight women—they paid for bass-thumping club mixes, then yearned for ballads that confirmed *a house is not a home when there's no one there to kiss goodnight*. In the late 80s, in Belfast, straight women were confused about the difference between what they wanted and what they needed. I was there to make money. I didn't have time for tea and sympathy. And I certainly didn't have time for mind games. When I was selling my body, I expected the customer to pay up. And not be stingy.

The gay escort agency—The Rainbow Coalition (You have to laugh!)—loved two things about me: 1. I was an arty student. 2. I had an accent. Both big selling points.

"We get lots of artists inquiring," the manager beamed. "You're bright. Cute. And that accent. . . . They'll love you!"

Grand, I thought. I signed up. I got regular bookings with a couple of men, a few nights a week. I had a steady income, work I didn't mind, and I had more than enough time to write and attend my writing classes—which, if I'm honest (and I am) left me bored.

When my Master-of-Fine-Arts friends found out about my escort work, the first thing they wanted to know was if I'd been paid to fuck anyone famous. The first rule of being an escort is not really caring who you fuck. What you notice, being an escort, is that most men don't really want to talk. And that was just grand by me. Silent men were my homeground. My Belfast was a city of partially hidden men, who only spoke to each other in hushed, wee sentences.

I would never answer the question about fucking the famous. Instead, I'd try to pivot towards something a little more interesting, and I'd say something like, "If you really wanna know, sex for money just highlights how much of our lives is lived inside our own heads." Because of my pivots, one of my have-you-fucked-the-famous "friends" christened me Padraig, the Philosopher.

Sarcasm from the innocent makes my stomach heave. After I was christened, I sauntered over to my fridge, peered inside to hide my face. "Yeah," I said, "Padraig the Prostitute Philosopher. The Triple P." Then I leaned further into the fridge, hoping for this nuisance to back out of my apartment before I slammed the fridge door shut.

So the truth is, in those days, I didn't have what you'd call honest-to-god friendships. The students in my program annoyed me. I found it impossible to be friends with anyone who had not known troops standing on the corner of the same road as the house in which they were born.

The men I had sex with, on the other hand, intrigued me. I had arrived in the U.S. already an expert in facial expressions; I could read the slightest movement of an eyebrow, a finger at a temple or a chin. My escortees' faces were alive with words, all of them unspoken. They were not interested in "sharing their inner dialogues." (Thank you, Jesus, Mary, and Joseph!) They didn't want to talk about sex. Or politics. Or art. Or any kind of angst. Did I care that a recent Nobel Prize winner for Literature on a New York visit paid me to fuck him? No. He never said he'd won the prize; I just recognized the perfectly trimmed white beard and those permanently grief-stricken eyes. I did not want to think about who he was because then I'd have to think about where he came from—his used-to-be country. Did I care that someone who'd had a whole room dedicated to his paintings at MoMa paid me to fuck him? No. Why? Because I didn't want to think about his life-size still lifes of corpses—depictions of his war-torn country. I felt about the famous what they felt about me—our bodies in bed together was strictly business.

My stories at the time were all about the same thing—death. My sex work never entered into anything I wrote. How the director of the program found out was beyond me. He never said anything outright, but it was there in his request that I escort (accent on the second syllable) to and from their hotels all the visiting writers that came to read their work—to audiences frequently more interested in hearing their own voices during the Q & As, than listening to what was being read.

In the workshops, I mostly zoned out when we were discussing the work of my peers. They were all young, writing the first hundred pages of novels, with parents and children as major characters, and usually some drug-taking scene, and some fumbled sex between a man and a woman. My stories had details like a car backfiring and the terror it instilled in my character as he walked the streets. Bombs went off. People died. And somewhere in my narrative there would be a scene with some sex—between men and women, women and women, men and men, sometimes between three or four characters—rarely on a bed, seldom in a house, and often standing up in an alley or a bombed-out building. The other students called my work "grim." Maybe they said "gritty." I forget. When it was my turn to offer feedback I tried to care, but I couldn't. I'd say stuff like, "I cannot think of a single way to improve it." I was not popular with my classmates. Nine times out of ten, I caught the subway home alone.

I thought studying writing was the opposite of joining the Peace Corps—an MFA was all about you, and the Peace Corps was all about others. Sometimes I thought of jacking-in the degree lark and going off to some war-torn country to help save someone else's people. It fucked with my head that I'd left behind Belfast and my friends only to fill my time with writing some good-for-nothing stories. But then I'd get a letter from my Ma with updates: "You know _____? She's in the family way." "You remember _____? She's about to have her second baby." And remember _____? He's a Da now—two little boys." Whenever I read these updates, I told myself that at least I wasn't adding to the problem by producing new lives for political factions to blast out of existence.

Sex for money kept me balanced, sane, and stopped me from wanting to take out my eyes in class. Plus, it was honest-to-god work, unlike being the English Department Research Assistant who spent days photocopying pages from books for some princely writer who'd gotten a shitload of money for a book about having sex with a sibling and—God forbid—enjoying it in a "complicated" way that took two-hundred and seventy-five pages to "explore."

After the director offered me the job of escorting our bi-monthly literary visitors, my two jobs became blurry. Even some of the straight men were game for a one-night "exploratory" trip in the sack. By the time this little part-time job had started I was already an expert on how to read a gay raised eyebrow that said, "I'm (a wee bit) famous and free for an after-event fuck." Or the straight male smirk that said, "I won't tell my wife, if you don't."

To the one woman they invited, I was practically invisible. She was in her sixties and still talking about her stultifying middle-class childhood. I wanted to put a gun in her hand and ask her to shoot me. But instead, I walked her back to her hotel and let her talk to me about Greek mythology and her garden.

I walked writers back to their hotel rooms at night, noticing how safe Manhattan was. I saw no evidence of the "No Radio in Car" signs of the recent past. I saw no reenactments of babies exchanged for vials of crack. I felt as if the images that American TV had exported in the 80s had lured me to the city with false advertising. This NYC was not the same one I had seen on cop shows, while sitting on a threadbare couch at home in Belfast. Occasionally, I'd see a heroin marionette strung out on the sidewalk, but they looked more like characters in a play, rather than real people in the city where I now paid rent.

Escort work helped me get a studio in Alphabet City, instead of living like a teenager in the university dormitory. My studio was so small that I called it my "stud." The bathtub was in the kitchen and it came with a lid, so it could double as a kitchen counter. When the lid covered the tub it was usually covered in breadcrumbs, greasy knives, sticky spoons, and splotches of jam. I didn't need cleanliness to keep me close to God. You only need to have your best pal killed in a bomb blast to know there is nothing godly imposing order on this earth. If God had proved his existence to me, I would have been willing to change my mind. But as of 1992, God hadn't.

Godless, I went to meet the visiting writers. The first one came to read stories about opera-lovers who knew good wines and took vacations in the Dordogne. (While he read, I fantasized about kidnappers taking him hostage and none of his family caring enough to pay the ransom.) The second writer came to speak about the history of genocide. In the Q & A, an audience member got into an argument with him about whether the pen was mightier than the sword. Genocide Man announced to his audience that pens aren't much use on the battlefield. (I can testify that they weren't much use during bomb blasts, either.) The third man came to speak about—well, I'm not exactly sure what it was he came to speak about; I think it was to be clever with words that seemed to be directed at no one other than himself. Which was also true for the next man who came to speak about the making of one of his novels into a film. Next, two poets were asked to read on the same evening. It was necessary to double-up the poets as this was the only way to get an audience large enough to make it worth the university's money. Both poets were disappointing. One of them confused jokes with poems, and when I expressed my disillusionment to the director he told me that I needed to read more of his work so that I could "get" what it was he was doing. The other poet was stuck in a different century, on a different planet—he rhymed and he rhymed until his couplets made me heave. To top off the evening, when most people had gone, Jokey Poet draped himself around a young student and offered himself to her by saying, "Lift me to your mouth . . ." Then he lost his balance, fell forward, and I was forced to stand over him, watching the Merlot drip from his chin. (If poetry completely disappeared from the world, would anyone even notice?)

The final visiting writer was the man who did not know the word for a peppermill and asked the audience never to tell him otherwise his creative world would lose its freedom. He also told stories—long ones with long pauses. He had traveled, lived in a few countries—for real, not just on a visiting writer's grant—which helped to lift his stories into something bigger, broader than they might have been if he had never left Boston. Even if his idea of freedom was seriously off, his stories did have a beauty to them—the devastating detail—that stopped me from zoning out.

To my mind, the visiting writer worth his weight in salt was Genocide Man. At the Cheese and Wine Reception, one of his friends said, "We all knew he was going somewhere be-cause in grad school he worked so much harder than everyone else." His hard work and his interest in genocide impressed me. But I had a question: Why did he jump on a plane to try to figure out genocide, when he could have stayed home and researched his own country's violent history? Then again, he had made it his job to look beyond what he already knew, and that earned him my respect.

"Are you saying that the sword is always mightier than the pen?" The pompous arsehole from the audience had kept hammering on at him during the Q & A, incredulous that this best-selling author would entertain such an idea.

Genocide Man fired back with, "Yes, yes, I am. What good is a pen when someone is about to lunge at you with a machete or is about to set fire to the tire around your neck?"

Though he had clearly lost the argument, the audience-arguer would not shut up. (I wished I'd had a machete to cut out his tongue!)

Of all the visitors I've escorted, Genocide Man was the man who needed me the least. Isn't it always the way—the man you wish would slow down to discuss life with you is the one who is busiest living it: *Sorry. Can't stop. Gotta go. Off to war. Off to take the machete out of a child's hand . . .*

On the short walk back to his hotel, he seemed distant. Maybe it was the exhaustion of performing for a crowd. Whatever it was, it was clear that sex with me was not even a consideration. But I was wishing he would say something. I wanted him to speak first; there was no way that I was going to intrude on his down time. As we reached the entrance, he looked at me for what seemed like the first time and said, "Northern Ireland, right?"

Anytime a Yank says Northern Ireland instead of Irish, you know you've hit on someone special.

"How long have you been gone?"

"Two years."

"The magic number. . . ."

"Magic?"

"Two years to adjust to a new country or two years before you can't take it anymore and want to go back home. Which side of the fence do you fall?"

"The first. There's stuff I miss about home, but nothing enough to make me want to go back. Anyway, I've come here for the opportunities. America. . . . Isn't it supposed to be the Land of?"

"Depends who you ask."

"Can I ask you?"

"Me? Then I'd say, no. It's the Land of Entitlement, floating in an ocean of ethnic hierarchy."

I knew what he was talking about; I'd noticed it as soon as I'd disembarked at JFK. There's nothing like a quick survey of who shines the shoes and runs the snack bars in airports for a swift orientation to see who stands on the lowest rung of a country's ladder. I waited for him to say more, but he wasn't going to add anything, so I piped up with, "I've left one fight. I don't want to get into another country's troubles. Not that it comes up; I know how to keep my mouth shut."

He looked as if he agreed with me, so I thought this would be the end of the conversation. I was waiting for a little pat-on-the-back final comment before he went inside, but instead he said, "Every country has its own brand of violence and its own group of outsiders. You don't have to write about your own experience. *I* didn't. I caught planes to try to figure things out. You've already caught a plane. Write what you want."

It was true. I had caught a plane. But I hadn't caught it to *go* somewhere. I'd caught it to get *away* from somewhere. Big difference. Maybe he knew that. Maybe he didn't. I wasn't going to bring it up, in case it made one of us feel like an arsehole. Instead I said something more appropriate for a Student of Creative Writing. "Here's my problem: I can't seem to stop myself from beginning or ending all of my stories with a death. But beginning or ending with death is cliché, my professors tell me. I don't argue when they point it out. Inside, though, I'm thinking, not where I come from it isn't. And once I've had this thought, I lose my impetus to finish. I think, fuck it. What's a poxy little story going to do for my people, your people, anybody's people? The pen, right, it's not mightier? It can't compete with a bomb. So I never finish. I've got a whole thesis of three-quarters-written stories."

Genocide Man offered me a cigarette. We each lit our own. He hid his behind his back, as if smoking it in public were prohibited. He let out a fast stream of smoke and when it dissipated he said, "You need to work harder, longer, deeper. Expect more of yourself. God knows *you've* got to because no one else is going to expect it of you. You've got the ingredients to be successful—you're a young man and you have Irish roots. That practically makes you royalty over here."

One of my first memories is running down the Falls Road to get away from the C. S. gas that the Black Watch was lobbing into our homes at the behest of the British government. I was six, holding onto my Ma's hand. She had my baby sister under her other arm, and as she dragged me she scolded me for not running fast enough. "Padraig, come on!" I was trying to keep up, but the gas was choking me and it slowed me down.

I know that people can't see inside your body to know your history, but any kid raised on the Falls Road would find it complete idiocy to think that simply by standing on American soil, he'd been reclassified as royalty.

By the time I was thirteen, three of my pals' dads had been killed, including Nicky's. Back then, older brothers and dads were dropping like flies. No one took us—the younger sons—aside to ask us how we felt or if we had anything to say. The only thing that we had was each other. After Nicky's Da's funeral, when everyone had gone, we sat in the graveyard and I held him as he wept. I kissed the top of his head in the way that I wished our fathers had done.

Wall Number One of the Peace Line divided the Falls and Shankill Roads at Cupar Street. Since it first went up in 1969 the Peace Line has gotten taller—yard upon metre. I grew up thinking everyone in the world had to be divided by a wall, otherwise the entire human race ran the risk of being killed while sleeping.

All the boys I knew went to Bobby Sands's funeral. Being there changed us. The stories of what happened in prison cells filled us with terror, but they also made us feel that maybe, just maybe, we too could grow up to become fearless. If Bobby Sands had starved himself to death trying to get the British government to submit, if *he* could write a book, sitting within the four shit-smeared walls of his cell, naked, writing on toilet paper and keeping it hidden inside his body, then maybe I could have written one story that mattered if I had not flitted off to New York, away from what felt crucial.

I stopped writing as soon as I graduated. I came out with a degree and not a single worthwhile story. I wrote nothing that stayed in anyone's head. I had tried to borrow the "every sentence is a camera shot" idea from the screenwriters, but I kept forgetting to pan out. Instead of focusing on the UDF or the Black Watch or whoever the fuck had lobbed the bomb, and why they'd done it, I'd lose myself in the small details. I'd focus on the still-standing fridge where there had once been a kitchen. I'd describe what was to its left—a baby's rattle, a portrait of St. Francis with a bird perched on his hand. Then instead of writing about the mother-of-four lying dead in the place that had once been her livingroom, I kept writing about the damn fridge—its door swinging open, a close-up of a jam jar, then closer—the raspberries inside the jar, then closer—the seeds inside the raspberries.

My Belfast was grey: grey sky, grey rain, grey summer. My Belfast was an empty house with the front door axed to pieces. Then another empty house with the door *and* the windows smashed. Then another. And another. Soon, I'd counted up to a hundred bashed-in houses. Then I stopped counting; not because these houses had come to an end, but because I was tired of it.

We smashed those houses—Nicky and me. We weren't princes. We weren't even footmen to princes. But we were smart—we knew it was better to smash up buildings than to smash up our lives.

One time, Nicky got his hands on some red spraypaint, "Today's the day, Paddy. We're gonna spray our mark on that wall—The Red Hand of Ulster."

"Nicky, man, you can't draw. Neither can I. And this is no joke. We can't fuck it up."

Neither of us trusted ourselves to paint the Red Hand with the respect it deserved, so we stuck to words. Nicky sprayed: *Belfast* . . . and handed me the can to finish. And in the color of blood, I sprayed *where the Emerald Isle turns red*. It was an odd thing to write on The Wall; instead of writing something about our allegiance, our faith, all I could think about was color.

By the time we hit sixteen the security checkpoints made us want to kill—ourselves mostly. Because the cinemas were all closed, Nicky and I would go to the shopping city to hang out, even though we knew it meant we would be body-searched at least once. Once we were inside, we had no money to do anything. We'd just sit around, warm and dry, talking about what we would do once we made it out of our divided homeland. Despite the everyday threat of walking along the wrong road at the wrong time, I still thought we would get out—together.

Life was shite. But Nicky made it bearable. I didn't want to fuck him. It wasn't that kind of thing. I just wanted to protect him, not only from killings and bombs, but also from anything that would take away our little bit of freedom. The trouble was that he was the kind of lad the girls went mad for—good to look at, not too shy, not too loud. At the time, everybody was fucking everybody else and the next day pretending not to remember. I tried to lecture him. "Nicky, man, be careful. You don't wanna be a Da at sixteen."

"Don't worry about me, Paddy. It's yourself you need to be minding. The girls are lining up for you. If you don't go out with one of them soon, tongues are gonna wag."

I didn't care how many tongues wagged. I'd watched too many overnight transformations—from virgins into fathers—to scare me off sex with girls for good. I was afraid that this kind of sex would muddy my plans to get out. I didn't even ask for blowjobs. I was afraid someone would ask something of me in return.

Sex for money was a clear exchange; it was the kind of trade I could handle. Have sex. Get paid. No need to see the person again. And later, working for the Rainbow Coalition had an added bonus—every man they booked me with was an opportunity for me to test out a new character. I began by trying on the history of someone easy—a recovering junkie. I was barely eating anything beyond jam sandwiches at the time, so

I felt like I had the right body to live this role. Another time, I tried on a would-be freedom fighter who never made it to the front to fight because of an accident in training. Once, when I was feeling a sick kind of nostalgia, I took on the character of soldier who'd been in the Black Watch. I never spoke about any of this role-playing to the punters; it was a backstory that I told myself so that I could make a note of the subtle changes in my behavior, which, in turn, made small changes in the escort/escortee relationship. I could never tell which way it would go with the client—if my backstory would provoke more tenderness? More punishment? A bigger tip? No tip at all? But still, it fueled me, kept me engaged.

Life—nothing tidy about it, nothing predictable. So much blown apart. And the shards are still landing . . . In today's paper, it looks like Peppermill Man has finally—after a twenty-five-year career—won a big literary prize. One critic called him a genius, another questioned the judges' choice. My shard of opinion falls somewhere else.

On the evening that I went to meet Peppermill Man in his hotel lobby to escort him to the venue, I had tried to make polite conversation, but he kept staring at my lips as if I were speaking a foreign language. Maybe it was my accent? I played it safe and stopped making small talk. It was a short walk—eight little blocks. Five minutes, max. The awkwardness wouldn't last long. But then he stopped to pick something up. As he bent down, a couple of pedestrian's stumbled into him. It was rush hour. The sidewalks of Manhattan were teeming. No one in his right mind would stop to pick something up unless it was a stockbroker's wallet. But it wasn't a wallet. It was a paperclip. He held it up to show me, then balanced it carefully on the top—the curve!—of a parking meter.

So . . . he had rescued a paperclip! And he had made it his mission not to know the name of a peppermill. Should this odd character have won this big literary prize? Well, my money would have gone on Genocide Man, but perhaps eccentricity is more important than political drive. Or maybe it was none of these things that got writers nominated for prizes; maybe it was how much hope and redemption their endings offered?

Redemptive endings are what most readers want, and at this, too, I failed. In college I tried, but I just couldn't. In my final scenes, my characters did nothing more than survive.

I'd left my country, I'd turned my back on my culture, I'd ditched my religion. And I had lost my best friend to the fighting. Two years in the program and not a single student had asked me if I was a Unionist or a Nationalist, a Protestant or a Catholic; not because they didn't care, but because they didn't know to ask. This was my creative freedom; not a blank space where the word *peppermill* should be. Maybe I *was* royalty, if royalty meant feeling free of where I came from.

The day after my sex-free escorting of Genocide Man, the Rainbow Coalition booked me with someone new, someone from abroad. He met me in a hotel bar that was on the top floor of a skyscraper. The whole place was constantly turning, but so slowly you only noticed it moving once someone had pointed it out to you, or if you happened to get a prized seat by the window and could, over time, see the changes in view. It impressed most people and that's why the Coalition always used this venue for their escorts to meet up with their out-of-town clients. But when you come from an occupied territory a rotating bar feels more like an insult to your intelligence than an attraction. In Belfast, people sit in the same seat in the same pub on the same street for their entire lives; the only new view they want to behold is peace.

I spotted my client immediately; he was the only one there who looked like he was waiting for another man. As he was the tourist, I took control. "Hi, I'm Padraig. From the Coalition. You wanna find somewhere else?"

"Hi. Plavko." He shook my hand. Formal.

"You wanna try a different kind of bar?"

I took him to the Fruit Palace in the Village. The brightly lit place accentuated his confusion at being brought to a juice joint. The walls and floors were decorated banana yellow, tangerine orange, and kiwi green. We sat at a strawberry Formica table and his gray turtleneck looked even grayer surrounded by this fruitbowl of colors. I ordered two Monster Green smoothies and brought them to the table. I put down the mossy-colored drinks. "I'm from Northern Ireland. In America, this means I must drink green drinks. Green equals Irish. You?"

"I am from Former Yugoslavia. I'm Croat. I don't know what color my drink must be."

"Probably red," I said. "Next time, you can buy us two Raspberry Blasts."

He laughed. And that's all it took. Two green drinks, followed by two red drinks, and we were instant friends.

Later, at my place, we got the sex over with. In the morning, we talked—war, occupation, and the countries we'd left behind. It turned out that having sex with me took pretty much all of Plavko's "life savings." He was on some kind of despair-ridden death wish. His plan: a final fuck before going home to kill himself.

"Jesus, Plavko! If that was your plan, man, you didn't have to pay for it. You could have just gone into a bar . . ." It was clear he wasn't thinking straight. I felt for him. I wanted to take care of him, offer him a hand. He stayed the night, then another, and pretty soon he'd overstayed his visa. I helped him find some escort work of his own, since anything legal was not open to him until he'd sorted out his immigration/refugee status.

Writers can use their writing for many things—the continuum begins at Noble Cause, moves to Revenge, and ends up at Sleaze. Whatever the impetus, the most embarrassing thing is using your writing to woo—for example, wooing past Nobel prize winners in the hope that you too will one day become a winner as well. At the time, it was transparent to all of us—faculty and students—that this was how the director picked the visiting writers, and we were all riveted to the spectacle; watching him waiting for the Nobel Train that was never going to pull into his station.

He was a sorry looking man—the kind who lied unconvincingly about his age and spat when he spoke. (Everyone quickly learned to stand back from him in conversations.) It was difficult for me not to be drawn into any scene in which he made an appearance. If he had grabbed someone in conversation, I slowed down to watch him inching closer as the listener backed away. His career was in decline—stories circulated about his poorly attended visiting-writer gigs at other, more prestigious colleges. After he returned from one of these disastrous gigs, he went from sorry-looking to making vicious attacks on the other faculty. By the end of my two years in the program, his colleagues didn't even acknowledge him as they passed in the corridor.

Perhaps the English Department faculty might have had more sympathy for him if instead of sucking up to previous Nobel winners, he put a fatwa on one of the previous winners' heads. Or better yet, masterminded a kidnapping—like taking a past winner hostage, and then sending a ransom note.

Dear Nobel Committee for Literature,

I am holding the current Nobel Laureate in Literature hostage.

My message is simple: I will release him unharmed as soon as I am named the next recipient of the prize. If I receive that middle-of-the-night phone call, then you will find him alive in the stacks of the New York Public Library (between Dickens and Dostoevsky).

Awaiting your speedy decision,
Pekelo Edmund

But this was my fantasy, not the director's. All that happened was that he came into the college less and less. By my final semester, the only time he stood in front of an audience was to introduce the next writer in the reading series.

One week away from my graduation, my stories were written, revised, polished most of the way through, but with failed endings—empty houses with bashed in doors, cars backfiring, crumbs left on abandoned tables. My professors had signed off on them even though they knew that they needed a lot more work.

All that was left was the graduate reading and the after-reading shindig, which meant mountains of cheese and crates of ten-dollar bottles of wine. The only difference was that this time I'd asked Plavko to come with me. Though I had made a point of introducing him as my roommate—which is exactly what we were at that point in our relationship—everyone acted like he was my lover. People were nice to him, bending closer, trying to grasp what he was saying. Occasionally, I'd walk by his attempt to communicate with someone, but he never seemed to get beyond, "Yes, Croat." "No, Croat." Sometimes we caught each other's eyes and smirked.

At the very end of the evening, when I saw Plavko leaving with Pekelo Edmund without saying a proper goodbye, my heart began racing. I was kind of caught off guard—this was my night—but I didn't hold it against him; at the time we both had to grab any opportunity that came our way to pay our rent. And honestly, I had already projected to the next day, and the soon-to-come details of the encounter took precedence over a reading that I felt mostly embarrassed about. Rather than subject myself to Plavko searching for some nice words to say in response to the reading of my failed story, I preferred the alternative: him back on our couch, filling me in with how his night had unfolded.

Which is exactly what happened. The next morning, Plavko pulled the knife out of the jar and began to slather his toast with raspberry jam, as I listened to his story.

So. The director's apartment was rich. Books, as you would imagine, were the dominant feature, and then sculptures from a bunch of countries from which he'd never set foot. Plavko—Mr. Art-Lover Himself—marveled at the varied display, and detailed for me what he saw. Wooden sculptures from India and various countries in Africa. Bronze and stone sculptures from Indonesia. Subtle and simple—beautiful pieces on pedestals and shelves with lighting that brought them to life. Plavko was then ushered into the bedroom, which he described as less like the bedroom of a man in his sixties and more like the den of a teenager—black sheets and a large poster, unframed, of a man Plavko could not identify, pinned to the back of the bedroom door. Edmund had used a magic marker to draw a red circle around the face to make it into a target. Inside the target there were a series of pin-prick-sized holes made from darts landing on the man's forehead, eyes, nose, and cheeks.

"You hate this man?" Plavko asked him.

"No. Just a game. Makes me want to write."

Edmund then got cold feet. He backed out of sex and settled for a blowjob. He was so drunk that as soon as he blew his load, he collapsed into sleep. Plavko, always in awe of luxury, fell asleep next to him on the softest pillows on which he'd ever laid his Croatian head. After about an hour, Edmund woke up from a nightmare shouting, "Fire in the rectum!"

Plavko just stared at him.

Edmund, fully awake, said, "I was dreaming."

After the bizarre outburst, Plavko decided to get out fast, leaving the luxury pillows behind.

I pleaded with him to describe the man in the poster. "Come on, man. You must remember!"

"White beard. At bottom of poster it say his name. Mikhail something. Maybe Russian. I forget. Sad eyes."

"Jesus H. Christ!" I wanted to wallow in this moment, picture it all, the declining literary star—which, let's face it, doesn't count for much, but still.... Target practice on another writer's face. I wanted Edmund's freak-out in the minutest details, but Plavko wouldn't oblige. He was not interested in this story; something more important was going on inside him. I could see the turmoil brewing—his eyes became vacant, his lips began to tremble, and right in the middle of this re-telling of the previous night's events, he plummeted into despair.

"What are we doing, Padraig?"

Oh no, man. Not now, Plavko. Please. I wanted him to continue. But he'd already surrendered.

"I lose my country, Padraig. I don't want to lose more. Yesterday, I stand on 14th Street and Broadway and I do not know where I am. People rush, rush past me, and I think of my neighbors back home: one door next to me, to the left, dead; one door next to me, to the right, dead. Is my luck two walls—one left, one right—to keep me alive? I ask my luck question to God, but no answer. Now I ask my luck question to you, Padraig. You have answer?"

I didn't.

We did what people do. We found a lesbian couple to marry. We went out on dates as a foursome. We took cameras to document every mock-heterosexual moment. Eventually, the Green Cards came through.

Plavko and I? We have no control. The people we once knew who were blown apart by bombs, or were driven into early graves by poison gas, or who disappeared from the streets, never to be heard of again, sneak up on us in the bathroom mirror as we are shaving, or on a knife-blade as we are making a sandwich.

I have my own questions, but I don't bother him with them. Whatever shard of my life I find lying on the sidewalk, I pick up without drawing it to anyone's attention.

I still have mornings when Nicky's face startles me in the bathroom mirror. When this happens, I try my best not to cut myself shaving. I steady my hand and I keep moving the blade.

How Now

The top shelf of the refrigerator is where Ekaterina keeps the lining of a sheep's stomach—cold but not frozen, ready to be unwrapped. Later she will cut the lining into rectangles, fill it with ground lamb, then roll it into finger-sized sausages. This stomach lining is white, which is also the color of the sheep's coat. The first time she needed a woolen coat was when she landed in this new country that wrapped her in a skin of coldness, one that required her to button up all the way to her neck. Though she had buttoned up, tuberculosis still found its way beneath the woolen collar, beneath her skin, and into her lungs. By the time she was given a hospital bed, the landlord had put her family's belongings outside on the sidewalk. "I'm sorry," he'd said. And perhaps he had been a little apologetic, but mostly his voice held fear. Ekaterina's mother, father, and brothers huddled beside their suitcases until another immigrant family across the street took pity on them and offered the family temporary shelter.

Pity for one another is something immigrants have in abundance, but they hide it from view. You cannot find pity tucked under an immigrant's arm, along with his newspaper, as he leaves for work in the morning. You cannot see pity in an immigrant's kitchen, in the pot in which she is frying the lamb with onions, parsley, cinnamon, pepper, and salt. You also cannot find pity in an immigrant's bootstraps. But it had found a home beneath the bra-straps that lifted Ekaterina's tired breasts.

The middle shelf of the refrigerator is where she keeps her sheep's-milk cheese. After removing it from the shelf, she will crumble it with a fork; its freshness making this easy to do. Then she will sprinkle the cheese with sugar and cinnamon, and wrap it in the finest leaf of dough. This cheese-filled dough leaf is called a *Dactylo* (a finger). After it is deep-fried, this leaf-finger will be the exact shade as her flesh-finger. If she is not careful she could bite into her flesh by mistake. But she's not worried about this—immigrants learn to be extra careful with all of their movements because their new countries have no tolerance for their mistakes.

This intolerance for immigrant mistakes is so palpable Ekaterina can taste it. When her estranged husband made a mistake, it tasted like raw meat on her tongue. As he packed his suitcase to leave, she said the words that were the most difficult to speak, "What has she got that I haven't got?"

Alkiviades had decided to swap finger-sized sausages wrapped in stomach lining for white bread covered in animal fat and sprinkled with sugar. He had also chosen to swap dough fingers filled with the sweetened cheese, for a pudding that is not a dessert but something filled with so much pig's blood the red becomes black. Though this new country's food does not welcome him home like his old country's food, he is too proud to admit his mistake. Instead, he continues to eat

34

the pig's-blood pudding that he finds in the refrigerator in the home that he now shares with his girlfriend.

Ekaterina does not want to hear the stories about her husband's mistake, but the immigrant grocer tells her anyway. "You know what that fool has done. . . . Of course you know he got her pregnant. . . ."

With each secondhand story he reports, the pity under her straps increases and her breasts feel even heavier. The news that her estranged husband is on his way to becoming a father makes her keep more and more of her words unsaid.

She stumbles when she asks the grocer, "Are these apples crisp?" The *sp* sound feels impossible to pronounce. She carefully parses English sentences before she speaks them aloud. If they include words with an *S* right next to a *P*, she keeps quiet unless the sentence is absolutely necessary. This lessens the amount she speaks. She develops a reputation among the new country's citizens for being stoic. The *st* sound is not as difficult to say as the *sp*. She can easily pronounce *stoic*. And since she can say it, she finds she can be it.

The immigrant families in the apartments above and below Ekaterina do not understand how her husband could have left her alone in a new land. Since they do not understand his leaving, they wonder if she is to blame. Her neighbors don't speak to her as often as they once did, so when she enters the silent building, she feels as if she doesn't exist.

Even if she hadn't received updates about her estranged husband's new life from the grocer, she would have still known that he existed. Last week she saw him with a newspaper under his arm. The headline read, "Pity The People," which made her wonder which people the world was supposed to pity on that particular day. Because the newspaper headline was so big, she imagined that the article must be pitying an entire country's population. As Alkiviades walked farther and farther away, though the headline was no longer visible, she thought she saw his body holding regret.

In her building, there is a rumor circulating that when Alkiviades left Ekaterina he took her stomach lining with him, and that is why her wedding band is still wrapped around her finger; it is what holds her together. Perhaps this is true, but perhaps it isn't. Perhaps, instead, what was lost happened years ago, before they married, when her body was damaged by the cold.

Before closing the front door for the last time, Alkiviades said, "You know why I'm leaving. This is my last chance to try. A last gasp." He snapped the suitcase shut and, out of habit, kissed her cheek goodbye.

After his departure, she sat in the dark for hours. At the end of the evening, she opened the refrigerator. Inside the illuminated interior, on the bottom shelf, was a finger-shaped pastry—once something special, but now no longer crisp.

*

On the top shelf of his refrigerator in his new home, sits something Alkiviades has yet to try—white, slightly soft, rendered animal fat. He sits at the kitchen table, watching his new-country girlfriend spread lard on her bread, then generously sprinkle it with sugar. As she bites into it, he watches the sweetened fat make its temporary home in the arc of gum that frames her front teeth. After finishing this slice, she eats two fried eggs, then washes this down with three cups of tea. Since the pregnancy her appetite has grown.

As she bends to kiss Alkiviades goodbye, for an instant, he does not recognize her face; she becomes a stranger, not the person for whom he has left his wife. After the door closes behind her, he worries that his choice to be with the mother of his unborn child has made his world too small. When the baby comes, they will be a family of three. With his wife, though there were no children, there were mothers and fathers and brothers and sisters and cousins and uncles and aunts.

He goes back upstairs and stands in front of the dressing-table mirror and repeats, "Ha-ou na-ou bra-oun ca-ou." He feels confident that he will soon be able to make his *ous* into *ows*. It is the *h* of the *how* that makes him stumble. He watches the mouths of the English: when they say the letter *h*, it is a slight breath, as if they were blowing out a birthday candle's flame, but when he says it, he feels like a windstorm fanning a house fire.

On the way to work, he buys another newspaper. On the front page a big war is over somewhere. Lower down the page, somewhere else a small war begins. He folds up the news, tucks it under his arm, and finishes his walk to work, trying not to think of the little wars he has left behind.

The foreman's name is Howard Brown. When Alkiviades arrives, he greets the foreman by saying, "Good morning, Mr. Bra-oun." Howard grunts, which is his version of saying hello. He does not try to say Alkiviades. This is an effort he is unwilling to make.

On Alkiviades's first day, Howard looked down his nose at this immigrant and spoke to him as if he were talking to a rat. "Thas a bit ov a moufful, in it? Les' call you Alki." The foreman bit into his roast beef sandwich. "Better yet, les' call you Al. Awright, Al?"

As he watched him chew, "Al" pitied the meat inside Howard's mouth.

At the end of the workday, Alkiviades walked along the street practicing. "Ha-ou na-ou bra-oun ca-ou." When he got home, he stood in front of the dressing-table mirror, practicing. "Ha-ou na-ou bra-oun ca-ou." He watched his mouth struggle with the words and began to loathe the sounds that he was working so hard to create.

His girlfriend walked into their bedroom, her hand tapping out the phrase's rhythm on her stomach. Then, easily, as if her language were the only language in the world, she said, "How now brown cow." By the time she'd finished wrapping her lips around the final *w*, a new little war had begun.

The Miracle of Timing

I don't mind getting up at 3 A.M. to bake bread for my village. Some people call it The Dead Hour—the hour when spirits come out, when nothing good can happen—but I think baking bread is a good thing, a daily miracle, so I guess I don't pay the Dead Hour any mind. My workday ends at 11 A.M., when I have delivered all the loaves to the village store. I do an eight-hour day even though I don't have to. I don't bake bread for the money. After my lover passed away, I was set for life. She died of liver cancer five years ago. She was a sensible woman, the kind who could be counted on to have her affairs in order, just in case a moose ran in front of her car while she was driving. But since cancer is a slower death than a head-on collision with a moose, she'd not only made out her will and named me her sole beneficiary, she'd also left behind a life-insurance policy that was large enough to pay off the mortgage and to make sure I wanted for nothing.

Having money in the bank is a blessing, but not having to worry about money when you're suddenly alone also allows you the luxury of time—time to wallow in nostalgia, time to feel sorry for yourself; in other words, too much time with nothing to do but grieve.

So I signed up for a bread-making course. It was supposed to be a time filler, something to do while I was figuring out what to do with the rest of my life. But you know how life goes—you think a choice is about one thing, then it turns out it is about another thing entirely. Turns out my passion is baking bread.

Someone who had the audacity to call herself my friend once said to me, "For a woman obsessed with baking you don't seem to eat much food." I cut off that quote unquote friendship right there. I walked out of her house forever and made it clear she was no longer allowed in mine. It makes it awkward if I bump into her when I deliver my bread at the village store, but I'd rather this tiny bit of awkwardness, than to have to listen to Ms. Lard Ass.

I carefully tally my calories each day. I am a small woman, so I try not to go over the hundred pound mark. If that happens, it makes me panic. On the occasions that I have seen the needle edge up to a hundred and three, it feels like a prick into action, and I immediately try to work harder. On these rare days, I bake even more bread. Just because I have to cut down on how much food *I* eat, there is no need for the other people in the village to suffer. I'm not saying that going without food is always about suffering. It isn't. Sometimes missing a meal is an act of salvation.

Take my mother, for instance. She is fat and her fridge is always stuffed. I don't think I've ever opened it and found room to add one more mushroom or cherry. In her house the fridge is all about plenty—plenty of this, plenty of that, plenty of everything. Frankly, for her, missing a meal every once in a while might well be an act of salvation, or, at the very least, might offer her less of the knee-pain that comes from being massively overweight. *My* fridge? Well, I keep a bottle of seltzer in it, some freshly ground coffee in the freezer, and my salad drawers are full of whatever fruit is in season. Right now, full of November apples I picked myself. Food tastes so much better when you work for it, even if it is just an hour of apple picking.

An orchard is my sacred place. I don't do churches. Sitting in a pew makes me feel like I've lost God, but picking fruit right off the tree or bush makes me feel like God is inside whatever I've got in my hand. When I bite into the fruit—it doesn't matter what it is, an apple or blueberries—I feel like I am taking God inside me. Not that kind of *inside me*. I don't mean anything sordid. I mean like eating something holy.

I have a real friend who has acres and acres of blueberry bushes. Every summer at peak picking time she invites everyone she knows to bring containers of any size and any number to pick blueberries until all of their vessels are full. I don't like to feel greedy, so I don't take along anything massive. I take one medium-sized black clay bowl and I fill it with blueberries. The midnight-blue berries against the black clay are gorgeous. Even when it's full, the bowl still looks empty.

At berry-picking time, I slip a handful or two into my mouth. It feels like I'm taking communion. For a wafer, I go home and I eat a super-thin quarter slice of my own bread. This is the kind of eating I've always dreamed of; not stuffing my face with greasy fat sausages before church, but slipping tiny blueberries in my mouth while standing in an open field.

On Sundays, instead of going to church, I have a friend over. He's been visiting me for the past six months. He's always on time. I love this about him. Years ago, my ex-friend mentioned to me that she took a seminar for high-powered business people and one of the things she learned was that if someone keeps you waiting for longer than twenty minutes, it is a sign of disrespect. It means that they value their time more than yours. I took this information inside me and I have not let it go. If anyone keeps me waiting longer than twenty minutes, it's the last time they do. Connection terminated. The good news is that my Sunday-lunch-friend is the most punctual person I've ever known. He arrives at noon on the dot. It's as if he has timed the paces it takes him to get from his home to mine.

Walking is a big deal to him. He had to do a lot of it to get here. He's a refugee. He was granted asylum. *Asylum* in this context means *refuge*, but I can't help it, whenever I hear the word, I always think *Welcome to the nuthouse!*

To get out of Niger, my friend had to walk across the Sahara Desert. On this grueling journey, he saw people die from broken ankles and sore feet. "At first, I slowed down to pay my respects," he told me, "but after passing the first four or five dead bodies, all their faces had the same look—no peace, only torture. This made it difficult to keep walking. I felt like the dead faces were looking up at me and begging me to stay. *We might be dead*, they said, *but we're still lonely*. Sometimes these faces looked like mirrors; in them I saw my own face. To stay alive, I had to walk quickly past. You understand?"

What could I say? I understood as much as I could. I hoped my face showed him that I was listening, that I had sympathy. I think he saw in it what I wanted him to see, because he kept talking. "By the time I crossed the killer Sahara, I had walked past 1,832 bodies."

He told me this back in May, when I first invited him over. We were still in the getting-to-know-each-other phase of our friendship, so I hadn't yet learned his long pauses. I thought he was done. But he wasn't. "Do you know what it did to me to walk fast, fast, fast, past nearly two thousand bodies?"

He was looking at me, but he was asking himself.

I waited. *One Mississippi. Two Mississippi.*

"It makes me dream the same dream again and again—I call it Death by Walking. But in my dream I stop. And because I stop I see the flies above the bones that stick through the skin. Each time I dream this it is not the dead, but the flies that wake me up."

What do you say to someone after they tell you something like this? I cut him a thick slice of my Sourdough, with a generous spread of butter, and handed it to him. "Here." When his teeth sank into all of that fat, I had to turn away. I'd had that butter in my fridge for a few days, leftover from a sweet bread I'd baked for someone's special occasion. When his visit was over, I tossed what was left of it into the garbage.

On his next lunch visit, he told me that before he left Niger he only ate food on the days when he didn't hear gunfire.

"Why is that?"

"Those are the days when the street vendors are not afraid to stand out in the road to sell what they cook."

"Oh." I said, "Maybe that's why Americans are so fat. Most of our food is inside, in supermarkets, and gunfire doesn't often find its way into the aisles. I'm not saying it doesn't, ever. I'm just saying it's rare. We float down the aisles with our shopping carts so full that the only thing we fear is how we're going to pay for what we buy."

Whenever he geared up to ask me a question, he would look to his left and to his right, as if someone were monitoring our conversation. His left/right eye-dart thing fascinated me. It slowed down the flow of our chats. But I didn't mind. I wasn't in a rush. After I said my thing about American supermarkets, he looked left, then right. Then asked, "Have you heard a lot of gunfire?"

"Me? No. Why?"

"You look like you are afraid to buy food."

I was still holding my kitchen knife when he said this. His question made me angry and I had the urge to lunge at him. *One Mississippi. Two Mississippi.* But a refugee does not play by the same rules as the people who are born here. So instead of lunging at him with my knife, and instead of terminating our friendship on the spot, I deflected our conversation. I wanted to give him a second chance.

"My mom's voice is like gunfire. Does that count? She's from Italy. Born there. Raised there. People talk loud in Italy. Not that I've been. That's what I've heard. Then she immigrated to New York City, which made her voice get even louder. Maybe it was to hear herself above the noise? And in New York City they're not so good with the pleases and the thank-yous. My mom learned that too. In our house, it was always, 'Didi, do this. Didi, do that.'"

"Didi?"

"Yeah, she called me Didi instead of Donna. I'm glad. Do you know how many Italian Donnas there are in New York City? How are you supposed to feel like you are a quote unquote individual when every other girl at the confirmation party—or every other woman at the wedding—is called Donna or Donna-Marie or Donna-Louise. No, thank you. I liked that she called me Didi. I just didn't like the do this, do that after she said my name.

"I don't mind being called Donna here. There aren't many Donnas in this little bit of Vermont. Lots of Susans and Susies. Thank God I'm not called Susie. Such a girlie name. If my name were Susie, I'd feel like I was never given the opportunity to grow up. Do you know the song? *Wake up little Susie, Wake up.* No, you wouldn't. Anyway, I think waking up is something that little Susie could have done easily. But grow up? Nope. For that, she would have had to become a Susan."

After I told him this, he called me by both my names. Didi-Donna. I didn't mind. It made me feel like he had extra affection for me. My fantasy of stabbing him for being rude dissolved. Water under the bridge and all that. As weeks passed, he learned to pick up on more and more American cues, like complimenting people on their appearance. He said nice things about my earrings or my hair.

After our first few Sunday lunches together, he didn't say any more about his past. Apparently he had told me the few things he wanted to share, and that was enough. Now we could be real friends. I baked him a loaf of Sourdough each week. The first thing he would do when I put it on the kitchen counter was break off a hunk, put it into his mouth, and with his mouth full say, "Didi-Donna, you are the best baker in America!"

When I realized it was going to become his ritual to do this exact same thing and say this exact same sentence each week, I looked for a way to respond without making myself feel too uncomfortable. So I would take a little bow.

When he showed up two Sundays ago at noon on the dot, I ushered him right in. "Sit down. Sit. Sit. I'll be right back."

He did not sit. Instead, he did what he always did—took off his coat and walked straight out the back door.

He found it hard to be inside. I never asked him why. If he wanted to tell me he would have. But I noticed how his face changed; it was as if he saw people hiding behind my furniture. And god forbid there should be an unexpected noise—a chair scraping or something—his whole body winced.

I pretended not to notice.

Once he was outside, he lit a cigarette and smoked it as if the journey from my front door to my back door was like crossing another desert.

In general, I don't like it when people smoke. But for him, I felt like every cigarette was saving his life. Again, I didn't say a thing. He didn't say anything, either. Not speaking was the glue of our friendship.

I had made us a special salad, something new—grated papaya, lime juice, and cayenne. It goes against my nature to buy a papaya—all those miles it took to transport it to my plate—but I saw it at the supermarket and I craved it. That's why I don't go to supermarkets often; it's just aisles and aisles of craving. I've learned to stick to the outer perimeter, which is not an aisle but a giant horseshoe. When I'm surrounded by fruit and vegetables, I can relax.

In the first weeks of our friendship, I took Saibou with me. When we got to the horseshoe that held the fruit, he looked distraught. "What's wrong?"

He pointed to the apples. "How can they be here? Now?"

"What do you mean?"

One Mississippi. Two Mississippi.

"Apples in May?"

How do you explain this to someone who has been granted asylum? Should I tell him this is the land of plenty where all fruit is available all the time? Or should I say, *Welcome to the Nuthouse!* I just shrugged my shoulders. We filled the cart with out-of-season fruit and out-of-season veggies. Then he insisted on adding cheese—full-fat Brie. Brie! I couldn't say I don't voluntarily buy full-fat anything unless it is to satisfy a client's order. My body was accumulating rolls of fat just walking to the checkout.

Now I feel awful. I shouldn't have used Saibou's name. He would've hated that. It's the name he had before he walked across the Sahara. He wanted people in the U.S. to only use his new name. One of the first things he did when he got here was change it. He thought he was giving himself an American name and no one in our village had the heart to tell him that here "Lemon" is the name of a fruit, not a man's first name.

Everyone smiled and greeted him with a good-natured, "Lemon! Good to see you." Or "Lemon, man, how's it hangin'?"

Two Sundays ago was a beautiful day. One of those days when late fall feels exactly the same as early spring. We decided to eat our food outside.

I put the salad in front of him, expecting him to remark on the papaya, but he said nothing beyond offering me his thanks. He ate the food so fast I'm not even sure he saw, let alone tasted, what I had put on his plate. I had cut my papaya into small pieces and was taking my time, savoring each mouthful. As I chewed, he found his voice, "This is a perfect day. Good food. Good sun. A blessing. Thank you, America! Thank you, Didi-Donna!"

One Mississippi. Two Mississippi.

"You are a good friend, Didi-Donna. I want to do something for you."

I couldn't really think of anything for him to do for me, but I offered to let him help me with my firewood. "You split," I said. "I'll stack." And after lunch, that's what we did. In silence—just the sound of his maul falling, just the sound of my logs stacking. After half an hour of this, I went around to the front of the woodshed and suggested we switch to give him a break. As I split, I got lost in my head, thinking of the breads I was planning to bake for the village in the coming week: French Seeded, Multi Grain, Maple Oat, a special holiday bread, and Lemon's favorite, Sourdough.

Once I had completed my mental list, I noticed the silence between us had grown. The logs had stopped being stacked. I went around to the back of the woodshed to see if Lemon was alright. He had fallen asleep, with a log tucked under his arm. Which seemed odd. So I knelt beside him.

He was gone.

If 3 A.M. is the Dead Hour, then 3 P.M. is the Perfect Death Hour. Because that's what it is—a perfect death—when you die on a day with perfect weather, after eating a perfect meal with a friend who sees you and loves what she sees.

Lemon's death was calm—a transition into a neverending sleep. His breath had gone out of his body, but his soul was still treading air.

One Mississippi. Two Mississippi.

I slipped the log he was clutching away from him and knelt close to his ear. "Lemon," I said. "I know you're still kind of here. Thank you for this perfect day. No more Death by Walking dreams for you, dear friend." I held his hand against my chest and squeezed it as hard as I could in case he could still feel me.

His soul took a step. Then another. And another.

Lemon's death was the complete opposite of my lover's passing. Ana's death still wakes me up in the middle of the night, in a cold sweat. I'm at the age where I can blame the cold sweats on my Change of Life, but I know that that's not what these sweats are about. Ana's death haunts me because of what I was doing—or should I say *not* doing—when she took her final few breaths.

I had run home from the hospital to take a shower, to get a clean set of clothes, some snacks, etc. But just as I was putting my leg into the leg of a fresh pair of pants, the doorbell rang. It was unusual for my doorbell to ring, midday, midweek. I threw on some clothes and ran downstairs.

It was my neighbor. "There's smoke coming over the fence from your garden into mine. Looks like something's on fire."

We ran straight through the house and into the back garden. There was smoke, but no flames. We were flummoxed. Then we noticed this home-décor piece hanging on the fence—a cast iron candleholder, with a spike in its center on which to place a candle. Except the spike was candleless. From a hook—perhaps to make the flame seem bigger?—hung a magnifying glass. The glass was slowly burning a hole in the wooden fence. It had already burned a little crater a couple of inches wide and an inch or so deep. My neighbor and I both stood there staring. He was probably thinking: *Why would anyone hang a magnifying glass so close to a wooden fence?* The answer was that Ana and I ate dinner outside as often as the weather would allow, and we wanted an outdoor candle. I thought this iron holder in the garden was perfect. But I hadn't given much thought to the magnifying glass . . .

Obviously, this smoky moment wasn't a major catastrophe, just a flare-up that was easily snuffed out. My neighbor left and I took the candleholder down. But the incident was enough to distract me from the urgency of returning ASAP to the hospital.

Instead, I sat in the garden staring at the hole in the fence. I peered into its blackness and lost myself in eleven years of shared memories—the good, the bad, and the one that stuck in my mind as the ugliest.

The little crater became a personal movie screen. I sat there watching the ugly: It began when I said, "Listen to this," and then read from the novel I'd started the night before—*Death with Interruptions*. This is what I chose to read to her: *Whether we like it or not, the one justification for the existence of all religions is death. They need death as much as we need bread to eat.*

I waited for Ana to say, "Yeah, so true," or something along those lines, but she didn't. She said, "That's crap."

We've all had that feeling when we are going along in a relationship and we feel like we're on the same page as our partner, then she (or he) says something so completely opposite to how we feel that we are tossed into a panic. This was that moment. Only it was extra awful because it was happening a few weeks after Ana's cancer diagnosis. I should have dropped the conversation. But how could I? I'd just found out that my lover believed in an afterlife. And I thought that I didn't. And she was staring death in the face.

I buried my face in my book. In the novel, anyone who is about to die—from sickness, old age, etc.—remains forever suspended in the moment just before death. I would never have wanted Ana to remain alive if it meant her life would consist only of the moment just before dying, always profoundly sick. On this, I was sure we would agree. Belief in the afterlife, however, was dividing us, and I didn't want any kind of division between us while she was alive. Death was the only division I would entertain because I had no control over it.

I searched for a place where we could meet, so I substituted the word *metamorphosis* for *afterlife*. As in, silkworms don't die. They transform. Into butterflies. There is no denying this. It is a fact. And if metamorphosis exists for a silkworm, then why wouldn't it exist for Ana? Transformation happens. I've seen it. Once I witnessed hundreds of butterflies coming to life out of hundreds of chrysalises, at the exact same time. The butterfly-birthing room inside the Museum of Natural History was transformed into an earthly heaven.

Since Ana's death, this miracle of timing is also why I fell in love with baking bread; all I have to do is add yeast, knead, and wait for the loaves to rise. Each week I watch hundreds of doughy miracles. All that is needed for this magical transformation is time.

But for Ana, in that moment, how much time she had was up in the air.

But we *still* had it and we could *still* share it.

Only I wish I had thought of all this before I said, "What might be crap to you might be someone else's point of view."

What was I thinking? Okay, I wasn't thinking. I was on autopilot, my words a teenage version of Marxism. I knew that religion was not just the opiate of the masses. Nothing about life and death was that simple. But there I was, solely responsible for putting the subjects of religion, death, and the afterlife, on the table, to be argued with my lover, who had just been diagnosed with cancer.

I couldn't put the words back in my mouth.

I felt sick.

She said, "So you think we need religion because of death. That's its sole reason for existing?"

As she was talking, I felt the bile rise to my mouth.

She kept on. "Okay, let's say there is no God and no afterlife, then what?"

I couldn't do it. I couldn't say: Death, Decomposition, Done. Even though, at that point, I didn't believe she was dying. Or, more accurately, looking back, I refused to contemplate that possibility.

She wouldn't drop the subject. My heart was racing. My eyes were blurring. I could no longer see the words to *Death with Interruptions*. I panicked. I blurted, "Nothing. Ashes to ashes." I didn't even say *compost*! At least if I'd said *compost* there would have been the hint of resurrection—the nutrients of one thing bringing something else to life. But no, I said *ashes* . . .

Fuck, I thought.

"Fuck," I blurted as I realized I'd been staring at the crater in the fence for almost an hour. I jumped in the car and sped back to the hospital.

But it was too late.

Ana was gone.

What was the last thing she saw? Not my face.

What was the last thing she touched? Not my hand.

I threw up on the floor by her hospital bed.

The taste of her death stayed in my mouth for weeks. I remember brushing my teeth, brushing my tongue. I remember brushing and brushing . . . What little food I ate tasted of nothing. Taste was gone. *Trauma* is what my doctor put it down to. *Sudden loss.*

In times of extreme despair my imagination runs wild. In the middle of this *sudden loss*, I started to imagine a world in which everyone who suddenly lost someone they loved was also deprived of the sense of taste. I saw mountains of food piling up and rotting. I saw thousands of restaurants suddenly going out of business. I even imagined a worldwide economic crisis caused not by a lack of food, but by the spoiled surplus caused by the large-scale loss of appetite.

Eventually, I got a grip on my life. Eventually, my sense of taste returned. Though it was completely toned down. I could taste flavors, but they were all subtle. Just hints: hints of blueberry, hints of apple. I chewed everything slowly, trying to coax as much flavor as I could out of each morsel. This slow chewing had a knock-on effect, which made my stomach shrink. Which then made me lose weight. Which then made me feel sick at the sight of people who obviously enjoyed food in great amounts.

Truth is, learning to bake bread wasn't all about filling my time. I also wanted to make something that sustains, and something that would not allow time to rush it. There is no rushing bread to rise.

By the time I'd become an expert baker, my appetite was lost. At first, people would comment on my weight loss, telling me it looked good. Then there came a point when the weight loss continued, but the comments stopped. Villagers who used to wave hello, and with whom I would exchange a sentence or two, would no longer look me in the face. Instead, I'd catch them trying to sneak sideways or backward glances.

When I was out making deliveries, I held the breadbaskets in front of me like a shield. This worked. No one came close. Except for Lemon, who saw a tiny woman struggling with a large stack of loaves. He took the basket out of my hands, and only after he had it in his grip did he ask, "You want help?"

He was already at the door of the village store before I could answer. I did my best to get across to him that I did not need his help, but his understanding of quote unquote basic English suddenly plummeted, and he used this as his excuse to ignore me and to cart the bread inside.

By the time Lemon inserted himself into my life I was grateful for the company. After a couple of conversations early on, he no longer talked about the pain in his past; so it stood to reason that he never questioned me about mine.

"No time to talk about the bad, Didi-Donna. No time." He took his last toke from his backyard cigarette and found something to do while I was finishing up the cooking. He swept. And with broom in hand, he began singing. Broom and song were united. I assumed the song came from somewhere in Niger. Perhaps from the mother or grandmother he never mentioned. I tried to find a roundabout way to ask him. "That sounds like a song from my childhood. Is it from yours?"

"No." He kept sweeping. His back to me. *One Mississippi. Two Mississippi.* "From my refugee camp."

That was it. No more details about the camp, just the sound of the bristles moving along my porch floor. He was determined to move forward with his life, and I knew that the biggest help I could give him was to share in his determination to look forward.

So when he died. In my garden. On my watch. With no one else around. Though I was devastated by the loss, I was also glad of this parting gift. He gave me this ending; it was mine.

I shifted his long, slim body as slowly as I could away from the woodpile, and I covered him in a blanket that was given to me by a Honduran woman I'd met on my bread-baking course. I'd simply helped her with the English language part of the exam and she gave me the blanket. "I made this back home," she explained, "to make something beautiful when everything around me was ugly. I give it to you for a thank-you."

I had never used the blanket to cover myself—it felt too precious—but covering Lemon in it felt right. It was a semi-shroud with a black diamond pattern that repeated. Once I'd wrapped him in the diamond blanket, I stayed by his side until the sun was ready to set. I wanted to give him one more thing as a send-off from this world into whatever it was that was waiting for him—an afterlife? Compost? Transformation? I brought out a small bottle of citrus oil and anointed his forehead and his lips. The smell of lemons surrounded us both.

What D - Y Equals

Who would have believed that ground chickpeas with tahini, garlic, olive oil, and lemon juice, formed into a paste, would be welcomed by the English general public and end up on a shelf in 1980s British supermarkets? Fotini certainly wouldn't have. She was so unaccustomed to seeing this product outside of her parents' home, she didn't immediately register it in the dip section of the Sainsbury's in her new London neighborhood. Though it was going to be a staple in the next stage of her life living with a vegetarian, she couldn't bring herself to buy it. In any home she'd lived in since leaving her parents' house, she'd made the hummus herself.

The tiny flat that she'd just moved into with her fiancé was going to be her *Something New*. After years of sharing flats with college friends, this was her first step into real adulthood, and she loved the idea of having her own home, sharing it with only one person—a future husband; someone who offered permanence, stability, and most of all, affection. She was looking forward to waking up with someone who would willingly wrap himself around her, instead of waking up to flatmates who'd just finished off the milk for her cereal.

Prior to meeting John, Fotini had one other longtime boyfriend. Their shared friends had all thought of them as a solid couple, but the truth was that he was a reluctant partner. Sure, they had done boyfriend/girlfriend things—movies, dinners, etc.—but they always did them in a group, rather than as a couple. It wasn't until it was too late, when the damage was done, that gulps of whiskey freed him to reveal that the reason they had socialized with three or four or five people at a time was so that he could palm her off on others while he continued on his hunt for his One True Love.

But Fotini did not stay alone for long. In less than three months, along came John. He had not only wooed her, he had also left his girlfriend to be with her. He had even proposed—twice! He seemed genuinely smitten. He drove her from one old friend to another to introduce her to all the important people in his life—best friends from college, ex-girlfriends who'd turned into pals. He had even driven his mother to Fotini's parental home to meet her mother. He had wanted their families to extend into one big family. Quickly. Though the speed at which everything moved disconcerted her, it also helped to convince her that this must be her own One True Love.

So when John rowed them out to the middle of a lake, and got down on one knee to propose in a grand romantic gesture, which made the canoe rock dangerously from side to side, she took the ring from him. Quickly. And said, "Be careful. Yes. Okay. Yes. We're going to fall in!"

When Fotini first moved in with John, she looked for ways to make her *Something New* feel like it was half hers as well as half his. On the bedside she put a black and white photograph of her mother and maternal grandmother before they arrived in England. She put the lace-edged linens that she'd inherited from her paternal grandmother into a chest she'd purchased at a flea market. But the real change, Fotini knew, would happen when her upright piano arrived. Once it found its place in this new home, she could fill the space with her music.

"Think of it as the *Something Old*," she'd suggested to John when he'd seemed unsure about putting an item as large as a piano in such a small livingroom. She arranged to have the upright carefully removed from her parents' home and brought up the narrow corridors through the equally narrow front door. When he saw how much of the small livingroom the piano took up, he seemed angry. She tried to remedy this by taking up very little other space. (One half of the bed, two dresser drawers, and a livingroom shelf.) She also stored her music sheets inside the piano's stool. In a further effort to limit the space she took up, and to bring back the look of love to her fiancé's face, she delayed her search for the *Something Borrowed* and the *Something Blue*.

The wedding was three months away, so each night she tended to a couple of the prenuptial requests on her parents' wish list. The wedding reception belonged to them; it was the gift she was giving them to make up for the fact that they had not arranged her marriage and that her future husband was not "one of their own."

Each night, after she had made sure that at least one of her parents' wishes had been granted, she practiced Chopin for half an hour before bed. In the morning, she practiced

Mozart until it was time to leave for work. This routine was helping her to feel at ease in this new home, which was still John's home, but was slowly becoming her home too.

Over time, however, she noticed that alongside her piano-practice routine, her fiancé was developing his own routine: he would leave for work at his usual time, early into her Mozart sonata, but he would return home for his dinner later and later, until one night he didn't return until fifteen minutes into Mozart, which was not night but morning. The previous night's chickpea stew was still sitting on the stove. He poked his nose into the pot, but instead of eating it, he went straight to bed.

As the nights leading to the wedding grew fewer, John kept practicing his invisibility. Two nights before the wedding, he'd perfected it—he completely disappeared. When Fotini woke in the morning, his absence confused her: was he actually invisible or had he simply not returned home to sleep? She tested her surroundings to see. She sat at the piano and began playing *The Raindrop Étude*. Fotini knew that he hated the dreamy sound of Chopin in the morning. If he were home, he'd come roaring out of the bedroom to scold her for waking him as he had done the first time she'd played a post-dawn *Étude*. Then he would do what he had done the previous week when she had asked him about his disappearances, which was to cancel out all the wooing, all the introductions to his friends and family, the proposal in a rocking canoe in the middle of a lake, by picking up the bedside photo of her mother and grandmother and throwing it at her head and yelling, "You are such a fucking bitch."

But after a few minutes of Chopin, John did not emerge. When she stopped playing the *Étude*, the flat was silent. But in this silence, she heard three slaps of skin-against-skin coming from the small flat next door.

In the last week, the neighbor-husband's slaps had become more frequent—at least once a day—and the neighbor-wife's sobs had become whimpers. The wife's crying disturbed her. She closed the piano lid and walked to where the sobs sounded closest. She knelt beside the baseboard. Resting her cheek against the wall, she touched its plaster with her hand. On her fingers she could still smell the garlic—the residue from last night's hummus. She stayed on her knees until her neighbor stopped crying.

When she got back up, her legs were shaky, but her mind was firm—she would not marry someone she could not see, someone who had called her a fucking bitch. She packed everything of hers that could fit into one large suitcase and locked the door behind her. As her suitcase bumped down the narrow staircase, she smelled the neighbor-wife's dahl. The scent followed her all the way to the exit. As she made her way to the car, she wasn't sure if she was imagining it or not, but she thought she could still hear her neighbor's sobbing.

She did not leave a note for John to say the wedding was off. She was sure the absence of her clothes, the absence of cooked food, the absence of her music sheets would be enough. She would arrange for her piano and the stool to be picked up later.

*

Fotini had always wanted the piano to be her instrument of joy, but it had never worked out that way. When she was a child, every time she sat down to play—Mozart, Beethoven, Chopin, it didn't matter which composer—her mother and father would ask if she could practice at some other time; specifically, while they were out. This presented a problem. Since she was not allowed to be home alone, it would be impossible to practice. (How was it that her parents hadn't noticed this?) She said nothing about this problem. Her father kept paying for the lessons. Her mother kept driving her to the piano teacher's home. Every Saturday morning, one of her household chores was to polish the upright; after which it stood, shiny but silent, with its back against the wall.

The piano teacher's instrument was a grand that had a sign on it that read: *Do not put anything on the piano.* The grand looked to Fotini like the still and dangerous waters of a Scottish lake. (The Loch Ness Monster had taken residence in every child's imagination.) When she was not playing the grand, she made sure to stand a safe distance away in case a monster jumped out of its lid. Also, the sign made her nervous. When she was asked to play the *Moonlight Sonata*, she imagined Nessie giving birth and a baby Loch Ness Monster crawling out of the piano's belly and plopping itself into her lap. Terrified of a baby monster landing on her, the fear made her playing even worse than it already was from lack of practice.

Her teacher scolded, "It is a waste of my time and yours, if you do not spend at least a small part of each day practicing your instrument!"

She tried to speak up. "Bu, but—" Words formed in her mouth, then they transformed into a paste that glued her lips shut. Even without this glue, speaking up was difficult. She could not say to her mother and father, "But I have to practice." She could not say to her teacher, "I'm trying."

The teacher did not indulge her stutter. "No buts. No excuses." As her foot pumped the pedal, and as her fingers dominated the keys, the teacher said, "If you do not practice, you will never have command of your instrument."

When her mother picked her up, Fotini kept the teacher's scolding to herself. She sat in the backseat of the car, looking for more monsters in shop windows. None appeared; instead, the gray, distorted English world blurred past.

This was the time in British schools when twelve-year-olds were introduced to Algebra and "The Irish Question." In Mathematics, letters represented unknowns. In Religious Knowledge, unknowns were represented by God. In Mathematics, there were equations to be solved. In Religious Knowledge, there was Sinn Féin. On the backseat of her mother's car, unknowns, equations, questions, and struggles for independence all got muddled in her head. When she got home, she tried to solve the piano-practice problem by using equations. In her Mathematics book, she wrote:

If x = piano, a = fingers on keys, b = at home, c = never alone, and if $x + a + b + c = d$, then what does d equal?

This bit of the equation was easy:

d = no opportunity to practice.

But then:

If d = no opportunity to practice, then what does d - y equal?

She spent the hour between the piano lesson and dinner trying to calculate the correct answer. The first time, d - y equaled an answered prayer. The second time, d - y equaled the separation of piano + pianist from family. The third time, d − y equaled government intervention and being placed in care (which, in effect, was the same as the previous answer). The fourth time, d - y equaled a struggle for independence. The fifth time, d - y equaled being swallowed up by the Loch Ness Monster—like Jonah and the whale—and living happily inside its stomach. Once inside the monster's stomach, she could repeatedly practice the *Sonata Pathétique*.

*

A week after her departure from her ex-fiancé's flat, Fotini hired two men and a van to pick up the piano and stool. She rode between the two men while they cracked jokes. As they entered the building, the smell of coconut milk and curried chickpeas called to their stomachs. By the time they reached her front door, the scent of her neighbor's curry made the van driver's stomach growl in response.

Inside, while the two men measured and experimented with the best way to remove the upright through the narrow space, she went to take one last look at the bedroom to be sure that she had left nothing behind. The chest was empty, but the dresser drawers were now filled with another woman's clothes; and on the bed there were more neatly folded out-fits—baby clothes; all blue.

John's proposal was the *Something Borrowed.*

The new lover's baby clothes were the *Something Blue.*

She dropped to her knees in her former bedroom and cried. Bach's *Toccata and Fugue in D-minor* pounded on the organ of her heart. On the other side of the wall, close to the base-board, the neighbor-wife could hear her sobs. The neighbor shuffled to where the sound of Fotini's crying was loudest; her ear pressed close, her hand touching the wall.

Silent is Help

In his *Advice to a Young Tradesman*, Benjamin Franklin says the way to wealth is dependent on two things: industry and frugality; that is, waste neither time nor money. Okay, so I might not be exactly what Mr. Franklin was thinking of when he wrote *Tradesman*, and I'm not exactly what he would have called young, but I have been industrious. And frugal. I have wasted neither time nor money. I am so far away from wealth it is not even funny.

I'm almost fifty. I work from home. I'm not in one line of work—I piece together two or three (sometimes four) jobs. At the moment, I have a vermiculture business; I'm a regular on Mechanical Turk and their Human Intelligence Tasks (aka H.I.T., aka online surveys); and I do some website design for small businesses. Does that make me a tradesman? It certainly doesn't feel like it when I'm sitting at my computer, sans either white or blue collar. None of my vermiculture clients is rich, but most have regular paychecks and health benefits. And none of the businesses I design sites for is a *Fortune 500* company, but most offer their employees retirement plans. (FYI: I have none of these things.) So when clients want to haggle over how much they want to pay for a box of earthworms or a new design for a homepage, I want to say, "I tell you what: you can have what you want for free if you pay my health coverage and rent this month. Fair exchange?" But I don't say that. Instead, I lower the price and look for volume—more customers, more clients, more Human Intelligence Tasks.

I'm industrious, Mr. Franklin, but you didn't mention what to do when not everyone's industry is considered equal.

When I sit at my computer all day, I regret not going to college to become a Park Ranger. I regret taking out student loans. I regret not getting married, not having children, not keeping a closer connection to my parents when they were both still alive.

At least I have a girlfriend.

I met Gabby at the dentist. "How long since you have your teeth examine?" I wasn't sure how long she'd been in the country, but her accent made me wonder how she'd found her way to small-town America.

"Can't remember . . . Four years? Possibly five? Six?"

She didn't give me a disapproving look and I was beyond grateful. I've lived long enough to notice that I am immediately attracted to women who offer me small kindnesses. I wanted to take this dental receptionist in my arms and kiss her forehead.

"Okay, please take seat. I call your name." Her voice transported me; I took my seat, closed my eyes, and saw palm trees on the inside of my eyelids.

I could also smell the detergent on my T-shirt. I was hoping she could smell it too. Maybe she would be attracted to a man in a freshly washed T-shirt?

Since my exam was only preliminary, I was spared one of those injections that make your lips feel like they've been inflated into an air mattress. I seized the opportunity to talk without drooling. I asked her where she was from, etc., and managed to pluck up the courage to ask her out.

Sometime in our first few weeks together I told her, "I will promise you my love and fidelity, but I don't want to do the living-together thing. If we live together, I can't just ask you to leave whenever I feel like being alone, since it would be your home too, and that would make me a complete asshole."

"Is no problem," she said. "Is only five minute in my car from my house to your house. I like it to be by myself too."

She wasn't at all offended. I was a bit surprised, but mostly I was glad that this conversation had gone so easily.

A year later, I'm turning fifty, she's turning forty, and I'm no longer sure that living alone is so great. I plan to talk to her about this change, about my regrets, etc., later tonight, after our company leaves.

Tonight, we've got "company"—i.e. neighbors, not friends—coming by for a "potluck." What a misnomer: a potluck does not require anyone to contribute their stash of pot or, if they've got it, their stash of luck.

I've lived in small towns all my life. This idea of being neighborly is not new to me, so I'm trying to be a bit more open to it for Gabriela's sake, but, honestly, it's all forced friendliness based on location. I don't want to know my neighbors. I don't want them to know me. If I have a heart attack there is nothing my neighbors can do to save me. Also, I don't need them to lend me stuff, as I make sure to keep my pantry stocked. I don't have animals, and I definitely don't want to cat- or dog-sit for any of their pets. Nor do I need them to keep an eye on my house, as I never leave it long enough for an eye to be needed. I don't want to deal with other people's bullshit. What I want is to be left alone. Which is also why I chose to study computer programming; it is a job I can do without other people around. But now the computer programming market is saturated and it is difficult for me to get the volume of work I need to pay the bills; hence my foray into the H.I.T. world and my earthworm enterprise.

I'm dreading tonight. I can see it now—the neighbors come over, the polite conversations starts: And what do you do, Matt? And I answer: H.I.T, web design, and worms. Where can a conversation go after this? That said, I'm sucking it up for Gabby's sake. She likes to be social. She wants to invite people over—to shoot the shit with strangers. And, bless her heart, she rarely inflicts any of this on me. But tonight is one of those rare occasions when she does, so I'm bracing myself.

FYI: I love Gabriela. Although, sometimes I feel like I'm stunting her life—social and biological. I'm beginning to feel like I've robbed her of the opportunity to be a mother. She never talks about babies—wanting them, having them—and I haven't wanted to raise the subject. Too scared of the answer, I guess. What if she said let's start a family—now? So I'm psyching myself up to a conversation about The Future—what she wants, what I want, what we might want to have together, etc.

Sometimes Gabby comes over while I'm working, lets herself in, puts on some Nicaraguan music and dances alone in my kitchen. When I watch her it's like each sway takes her back to a specific moment in time—deep in her past, deep in her country. I wouldn't join her even if I did feel the inclination to get up. She dances in a way that says *this music belongs to me and don't you come near it.*

I give her privacy to remember her homeland and whatever she left behind that she still wants to remember.

One day last week, the neighbor to my left and the neighbor to my right cornered her as she pulled into my driveway. Together they managed to finagle tonight's potluck.

"I say I make chicken," Gabby shouted over the music blaring from the kitchen. "Everybody love chicken. The lady who works at the yoga studio—Helen—said she bring a salad. And the other lady who works at the nursery—I forget her name . . ."

"Caroline."

"Yes, Caroline. She say she bring a pumpkin pie. Do you have six plates?"

"Six?"

"Their sons are coming too."

And there you have it: two divorced, health-benefitted (one of them mortgage-free) mothers are coming over with their teenage sons in five hours. Awesome. Which will interrupt my routine of working till I drop and then joining Gabby on the couch to watch TV until we both fall asleep.

When I found out about the plan to invade my home under the pretense of being neighborly, I gave Gabs $20. "That's for the chicken and the few bits you think we'll need. It's my last twenty, Gabs. Go easy, if you can."

"No worry. I make it work."

Even after a decade, American supermarkets are still a novelty to Gabriela. She loves to spend time wandering up and down the aisles, amazed at the variations of one particular product. After each trip, she updates me. Three days ago she came home with a grocery bag under each arm, bursting to tell me about her latest supermarket discovery.

"Guess what kind of hummus they invented? Guess!"

"Chicken Liver hummus."

"No, estupid."

"Rabbit hummus."

"No. Think!"

"You want me to think about hummus? I've only got one life, Gabs."

She looked disappointed that I wouldn't play the Guess The Latest Supermarket Product game.

"Pumpkin hummus. For Halloween! Awesome!"

FYI: When Gabriela says *awesome*, she means it. She is in awe of this culture—its need to always invent something new to be bought: the multitudes of breakfast cereals, the scores of cookies and crackers, the multiplicities of jams and jellies, the infinite variations of sugar and artificial sweeteners. And yesterday she was in awe of another variation of hummus.

Gabby is sincere; she doesn't do sarcasm. She leaves that for me. I also shovel the snow out of her drive in the winter and keep up her yard in the summer. In return, she does my food shopping whenever I feel like the bright lights and hard sell of supermarket aisles are too much for me to bear. This exchange of domestic duties keeps us both happy; neither of us has the money to pay others to do domestic stuff for us, so barter it is. Industry and frugality, Mr. Franklin, reign supreme around here.

She took the $20 from me and said, "Thank you, master, for your big generosity," and then she rolled the twenty-dollar-bill into a cigarette-sized tube and pretended to smoke it. Pretending to smoke is Gabby's version of impersonating a person of leisure. For me, it is just another way to get through a few more minutes of a thankless workday. As she flicks the imaginary ash from her imaginary cigarette over her beautifully real shoulder, she says, "And after I buy chicken, would you like me to cram it too?"

"*Stuff* it, Gabs. *Stuff* not *cram*. But I will happily cram you."

She pulled me into the bedroom.

We like to joke around. We're probably a bit too raunchy for our neighbors, especially Helen, the yogi. She looks like she hasn't been crammed in a long time. I can't imagine who'd want to volunteer his services to someone who looks like she can't even spell the word *fun* let alone demonstrate its meaning. I'm guessing that after the final reverberation of *OM* dissipates into silence, Helen collects twenty-dollar bills from the stay-at-home moms and probably puts them straight into some high-interest retirement account. I can tell you this, her one-hour yoga classes every Monday, Wednesday, and Friday don't pay for her annual winter trip to Hawaii. It isn't industry and frugality that helped her amass her little fortune; it was marrying the manager of a large bank.

You have no idea how the world has changed, Mr. Franklin. There is now something called "disposable income." This is not supposed to mean money you flush down the john, but it has come to mean that. Plenty of people are adding to their credit card balances with The Clapper. *Flush.* The Swiffer. *Flush.* And, wait for it: Whack Off—the insect repellent "as used by the

Armed Forces." *Flush*. I don't have any "disposable income." Any money left after paying my bills, instead of purchasing Whack-Off-The-Clapper-with-The Swiffer, it goes into my account for necessities like new snow tires or wood for my stove. It makes no difference, Mr. Franklin, if my creditors hear "the sound of my hammer at five in the morning or nine at night," or if they hear my voice "in a tavern when I should be at work." I can be as lazy or as industrious as I like. There is only one thing that stops 21st Century creditors—frugality in service of monthly payments.

You wanna talk frugal, Mr. Franklin? Okay, let's talk frugal: wood costs less than oil. I buy my wood green, which means that it is not yet ready to burn. Green wood costs less than seasoned wood that is ready to be tossed into the fire. Buying green wood far enough ahead saves me $75 per cord. In the 21st Century this is abso-fucking-lutely frugal.

It is precisely because Gabby and I don't have any disposable income that most of our nights are spent watching TV. Though I guess you could say this is not being industrious. Mostly, we watch American programs that focus on crime. We watch young, poor, unemployed men committing offenses—often killing other young, poor, unemployed men—getting caught and going to jail.

Last night's young man was in a police interview-room howling like an animal caught in a trap. He was afraid to speak about the shootout he saw because he thought it would mean the end of his own life. He dropped to his knees and said to the detective, "*You* can go back to your nice house. But *I* have to go back to my apartment building." His forehead kissed the floor. At first, I thought he was praying, but then

I saw his tears. "They're gonna come for me, man. They're gonna kill me."

The detective could not argue. He was a good man. "Get up, Mikey." He offered young Mikey his hand to help him up off his begging knees.

At the sight of this, Gabriela began to weep. When she saw me looking at her, she said, "Sorry." Then she put her arm over her face to block the screen. When I turned down the volume, her sobs sounded louder. I put my arms around her and felt her tears through my T-shirt. "No need to apologize to me, Gabs. Our justice system makes a lot of us cry."

"He is someone's son, you know. Someone's child."

"Yep, Gabs, I know."

I got up.

"Where are you going?"

"Google." When emotion is this raw, I'm lost.

"Google?"

"I want to find statistics on poverty and wealth in the U.S."

You don't have to be a Wiz on the World Wide Web to find this kind of statistic. It is there for us all to easily access, should we ever decide to rise up in revolt.

Google obliged me. I wrote down the statistics, then I broke the data down into an easily digestible calculation that I could share in casual conversation on the rare occasions that I leave my house. Like this morning, when I drove to the post office.

"Did you know," I said to the post master, "that if the U.S. had 100 dollars to share with 100 people, 20 people would take—and I do mean take—84 dollars, and the other 80 of us would be left—and I do mean left—with 16 dollars?"

I could tell that my statistical conversation had made an impression on him, but it wasn't enough. I wanted him to take his eyes off the screen attached to the weighing machine, to look at me, and to raise his fist in a gesture of solidarity, or at the very least to raise his eyebrows to reinforce his disgust at the inequity. So I broke it down some more.

"Do you know what that means?" I said, casually rearranging the paperclips strewn on the bit of countertop closest to me. "It means that *we* get 20 cents each and those other 20 people get twenty-one times that amount. *This*. . . ." My voice got slightly louder, my facial expression more self-satisfied because this new breakdown did indeed have the desired effect. He was now facing me, impressed by my knowledge and, possibly, by how neatly I had formed the paperclips into a pile, thereby giving order to his work area. "*This* is how wealth is *not* distributed in the United States of America . . ."

"Yeah," he said. "Yeah."

We shook our heads in a united gesture of loathing for the people who had twenty-one times the amount of money we had.

Then he looked at the person behind me and said, "Next."

I felt cut off. I hadn't yet had the chance to put away my change. I swept up the coins, adding the pile of paperclips in the process. Without one iota of guilt, I slipped the lot into my backpack. I got back in my car and tried to calculate how much money I could save, and how much free exercise I would gain, if I were to leave my car in my driveway and walk the two miles to and from the post office. The roundtrip journey would take me approximately forty-five minutes to an hour, depending on how many people were ahead of me in the post-office line, and how long each person ahead of me opted to chat.

Aside from the second-home owners who live in my town on weekends and national holidays, the majority of the full-time population is comprised of retirees who have chosen not to move to Florida to live their last days in the heat. Instead, they employ young men to rake their lawns in the fall and to shovel their drives in the winter. But in the spring and summer months, they are happy to putter about in their front gardens and back yards, planting and weeding. But when these retirees don't have their spring and summer gardens to wile away their days, each trip to the post office becomes an opportunity to fill their time.

With this knowledge, I try to plan my trips to the post office when I think the over-seventies are most likely to be home making scrap albums filled with the sanitized versions of their lives to leave to their grandchildren. But five times out of ten, I still find myself standing in line behind an old man who wants to tell Postmaster Bobby how playing his cornet in the brass band has given him a second lease on life. *Come on, come on*, I'm thinking. *Some of us are still on the clock. I have a mountain of H.I.T.s waiting for me.*

Because I often get my timing wrong, I factor that my trips to the post office can take up to an hour. On the days when this happens, I force a smile on my face to hide my gritted teeth. FYI: My hourly rate, plus gas for the car, works out to approximately $30, so this trip could cost me as much as thirty bucks per day, and that is more than what I spend for an entire week's worth of gas. But if I walk to the post office the time it would take me would double. Due to this calculation, driving feels like a thrifty alternative to walking. So I fire up my Volvo feeling frugal.

Last night Gabby and I watched a documentary that focused on a working-class home in India where one boiled egg at dinner was the special part of the meal; so special, there was not enough money to provide one egg for each person. The one egg was given to the guest. (Irony of ironies—an American.) The rest of the family went without. That TV egg stuck in my mind.

Before I drove home from the post office this morning, I stopped off at the store and bought a dozen eggs. I also bought a pumpkin. This purchase cost me a total of $10.50. For the family in last night's documentary, $10.50 was more than the head of the household's daily wage. I felt wasteful buying a food item that was not for eating, but Gabriela had asked me to haul home a pumpkin so that she could carve it before our potluck-neighbor-guests arrive.

Though I am a New Englander, I've never carved a pumpkin. This was Gabby's idea. She wants to take part in as many American excuses to celebrate as possible. It's partly about wanting to belong, but mostly it's because she wants to take every opportunity to celebrate the fact that she's still alive.

Bad things happened in Nicaragua.

On rare occasions, out of the blue, she will volunteer a small scene (never an entire story) from her life. Whatever anecdote she shares with me usually ends on something I don't recognize as an ending. It's always the same: she finishes what she has to tell me—last time it was about the death of her eldest brother, a dockworker killed by an underwater landmine planted by the Somozistas in the Port of Corinto—and at first I'm silent because I don't realize it's the end, and then I'm silent because I realize it is.

Gabby doesn't give me details. Like if her brother was a Sandinista. Like if he was married. Like if he had kids. She only relates the climaxes of her stories. No lead-ins. No endings. Just a short build-up to some devastating fact. I don't quiz her. I don't ask for more. I figure she will tell me if she wants to. And if she doesn't, it's her choice and that is good enough for me.

We all have things we want to forget.

Neither Gabby nor I want to talk about our past. We each want to be left alone inside our own head. For example, what good would it do her to know that my ex asked me to give her the money to abort another man's baby? (A pregnancy that happened after I'd proposed to her . . .) I gave her the money I'd put aside for the following year's wood, on the condition that she immediately move out. As soon as she was packed, I put the money in her hand, and I took a long drive while her friends loaded up the moving van.

The following winter was long and I had to go easy with the woodstove. Every piercingly cold night cut into me. After that, I wanted everything to be mine—my home, my feelings, my money.

Gabby and I are happy living on our own little islands of the unspoken, and because of this we're also willing to indulge each other when one of us requests something that the other wouldn't normally do. Such as carving a pumpkin before the neighbors arrive. As we stood with knives in our hands, I said, "Let's carve a scary face and put a light inside it to keep away evil." My own face took on a devilish sneer at my suggestion.

"Maybe if we make the face really scary we can frighten them away and the potluck will be canceled."

She turned up the music to block me out.

"I can't hear you. Turn it down."

"I say why you complain? Is just a bit of food, a bit of guests. They are not going to move in your house."

"It's not that, Gabs; it's the talking just to talk. If I wanted to talk to someone about something worthwhile, the only person I'd choose would be you."

"Is does not have to be important talk. You like watching cop shows, yes? So why you don't invent like you are the detectives on TV? Instead of the potluck, you can invent you are on a mission."

"*Pretend*, Gabs. Not *invent*. You just love yourself some pretend, don't you?"

I picked up my bird-watching binoculars and peered into her eyes. Close up her face looked different, like she had special powers that could tell what I was thinking. I didn't want her to get a whiff of the after-dinner-chat I was planning until I was ready to spill, so I put back the binoculars and kept the conversation where it had already landed.

"Why would I want to find out our neighbors crimes? I'm not interested in their misdemeanors. I'd rather be on a mission to hack into their retirement accounts."

"Okay, do that." The idea of me committing a white-collar crime was inconceivable to Gabby. "You try to hack out their retirement information and I try to find out their little crimes." She was highly amused at her own joke. "Deal?"

"Hack *in*. Not *out*."

Helen, the unhappy divorcée and yoga teacher (plus son) came towards my house from the left (with a big bowl of salad) at the exact same time that the shell-shocked divorcée and first grade teacher, Miss. Caroline (plus son) approached from the right (with a huge Tupperware bowl of something that looked like soup). Helen had dressed up for the occasion—sleek black clothing and silver bangles that announced her arrival. I watched her heels try to navigate the uneven parts of the road. Caroline, on the other hand, looked like she had just come from a play date with a bunch of five-year-olds—blue coveralls, red top, red shoes, and a yellow headband that pushed back her curly blond hair. Both sons trailed a step behind their mothers. Helen's son was dressed in some anti-fashion assortment of secondhand clothes. Caroline's son towered over his tiny mother. His frail body and thick mop of black hair made him look like an elongated chickadee.

Gabriela was on the doorstep, turning the pumpkin's scary face towards the neighbors to my left, but it did not stop their approach. I stood frozen in the doorway. Trapped on the threshold. Praying that this orange overgrown fruit would live up to its reputation to scare away evil.

But the dinner guests kept advancing. *Awesome.*

There was a flurry of welcome with Gabriela shocking both women and their teenage sons by depositing kisses on each of their eight cheeks. Kissing your neighbors in our town is not the usual custom.

I love it when Gabby shocks people with something un-American. One of the teenage sons grinned and the other one wiped his cheek, then immediately looked embarrassed for having done so. The two mothers quickly replaced their looks of surprise with looks of nonchalance, as though kissing the neighbors was what they had come to expect living in small-town U.S. of A.

Gabriela is still a constant source of surprise to me. Sometimes she is so painfully aware of every detail that I wonder how it's possible for her to walk down the street. At other times, it's as if her hyperawareness has an automatic dimmer and she becomes oblivious to even the most obvious details—be they expressions of shock (the mothers) or delight (the boys).

Early on in our relationship, when I first pointed out this difference in her reactions, Gabby said, "This is because I come from *tierra caliente*—the land of forty volcanoes! Sometimes I am liquid, sometimes I am ash."

To be honest, I don't always know the exact connections Gabriela is making but usually I kind of get what she means. Which is enough for me. I don't want everything explained.

The teenage sons were still behind their mothers. I felt for them. They looked like mini versions of me. I wondered how much guilt-tripping had gone into getting them to accompany their moms on this visit. I mean, what teenage boy wants to go to a potluck with his mom at a neighbor's house? They must have drawn from some special reserve, designed for when sons have to buoy their moms after their dads have split.

"Come in. Come in." Gabby became instant host. I was happy to be relieved of this duty, even though it was my doorstep she was welcoming them over. The women chatted. The boys sat silent. I thought about talking to the boys about vermiculture, but instead I just listened. Then we all moved to the table, where each guest was offered the same amount of food. Unlike the documentary on the distribution of eggs in Indian homes, all our plates were identical, except for one of the sons who did not eat meat. In lieu of chicken, Gabby forced him to have extra potatoes, which he gladly accepted. Once the chewing was well under way, and Gabby had successfully lowered everyone's guard with kisses and extra vegetables, she lunged in for her version of polite conversation.

"So Helen, you are mating now?"

Awesome. That's my girlfriend!

About eighty percent of the time Gabby gets her words right. But then there is that free-floating twenty percent where the wrong word is slotted in, and if we are in public, I hope it won't cause too much confusion or embarrassment. Helen acted—reacted?—as if she had a vice squeezing her skull; her cheeks kind of squished together, which caused her eyebrows to curl upwards. Caroline's son was squirming. And so was I. Helen's son gave a quick snort and kept shoveling food into his mouth.

Gabriela caught my mortified expression. I caught a slight (unperturbed) shrug of her shoulders. Then she miraculously corrected herself.

"Dating, I mean."

Helen's distorted face, and the concomitant signs of embarrassment, forced her son to quickly jump in.

"Oh yeah, Mom's dating my math tutor. First he comes by to confuse me with equations, and when he's done he takes Mom out for Italian. They bring me the leftovers. I love it. Aside from her yoga classes, it's the only time I'm in the house alone."

Helen kept chewing her salad. (Such industry.) In fact, her chewing got slower and more pronounced as she worked towards finding exactly what she wanted to say. (Such frugality.)

"Well, I wouldn't call it dating, exactly. We've had a couple of meals and—"

"Kisses when he brings you home?" Gabriela coaxed.

"No, no kissing. Like I said . . ."

"No kissing? But everyone needs kissing." Gabriela elbowed Helen's son, coaxing him to join her in goading his mother.

If God or Satan exists, please kill us all now.

Helen was caving; her shoulders were curling in, as if she were trying to protect her body. I did not want to be forced into noticing stuff like this. I just wanted to be left alone. I wanted these Potluck People to leave. I wanted the whole world to remain outside my front door.

Sometimes I watch TV in the middle of the day when I should be doing an H.I.T. or packing earthworms or industriously building a new homepage for the KlownsForKidz site. Because I'm alone, with unfettered access to daytime TV, I find myself staring into the faces of female guests on talkshows, listening to their concerns, their obsessions, and whatever else occupies their dissatisfied minds. I know what I see is skewed—a certain kind of America—but frankly, Mr. F., industry and frugality are not what they are talking about. I'd go as far as saying that these two things wouldn't even make their Top Ten Lists of Major Preoccupations. They go on TV to get help, but when they get there they wear their words like a disguise, hoping someone will care enough to discover this about them. They want to be seen.

Some of these talkshow women are using yoga to rid themselves of this camouflage. One woman—physically attractive, with a voice that made you want to lean in closer to the screen—was unforgettable. It wasn't her beauty or her voice that made me take notice; it was that she had let down her guard. "My yoga class is the only time I'm ever touched. When my teacher corrects my posture, her hands on my spine feel like love." Instead of the applause of agreement, the audience responded to her comment with a stunned silence.

Helen was a woman who wanted to be lovingly touched, someone who had a bit of herself missing. It wasn't what *we* thought was missing; rather it was what *she* thought was missing—a gaping hole made by her husband walking out after seventeen years of sharing the same bank account, the same refrigerator, the same bed. It wasn't only me who saw her this way; it was also her son. Poor kid. On his face I could see the mark of witnessing too much of his mom's loneliness. He wanted her to hook up with someone for his sake as much as hers. He loosened the skinny leather belt that was acting as a necktie, and said with gusto, "Yeah Mom, I think you should go for it with Mr. Freeman. He's not like the other teachers. He's traveled a lot. He's always telling us stories about his adventures. He's even been to India!"

"I know he's been to India. I know he's traveled—"

Helen squinted when she said the word *traveled*. I'd never noticed how expressive her face was before.

Caroline hadn't joined the conversation since Gabriela had asked Helen about mating. She looked like a suburban deer caught munching on a rosebush—wanting to bolt, but enticed by the forbidden bloom before her. She saw me looking at her and responded to this by knocking the chicken drumstick out of her son's hands, then saying to him, condescendingly, "Use your utensils."

Who *was* this little woman who took care of kids? I couldn't tell if she was a saint or a sinner. I tried to pretend like I was some reality TV detective on a mission, but I was thrown off by the display of Helen's raw emotions. Caroline's only crime this evening, as far as I could detect, had been a misdemeanor—talking to her teenage son like he was in first grade. Her son snapped to it and picked up his fork.

Everything about this boy said *Good Kid.* Not an ounce of teenage rebellion in his body. This worried me. When the rebellion doesn't show up on time, it makes me wonder when and how it's going to surface. I fought images of him as a balding forty-year-old in a clearing in the woods, making an altar to Satan. I imagined an investigative journalist wandering along a night path, lit only by a large moon, talking quietly into his mic, promising his TV audience that what they were about to see was a sampling of an ever-growing devil-worshipping trend, spreading throughout small New England towns at an alarming rate. Then the camera would pan out to Caroline's middle-aged son, mumbling his prayer to the Dark Forces of The Night.

But this was a fantasy of the future, and the only dark forces of the night currently present were the ones that had conspired to group these women around my dinner table to worship at the Altar of Neighborliness Going Horribly Wrong.

Had Helen ever committed a crime? A misdemeanor? I doubted it. I'd pegged her as the sort that tried her best to live up to other people's expectations, rather than what she wanted for herself. (Is this a crime?) But she did have a story. I read it in the way she had emphasized the word *traveled*. Her husband had left her for, yes, a younger woman, but it wasn't so much the age difference as the fact that The Other Woman was a Spaniard with her own vineyard. Helen's husband could not resist the romance of it. He was barely on the plane, on his way to a vineyard a hundred miles out of Madrid, before his fifteen minutes of small-town-fame had begun. Even Postmaster Bobby had a comment. "Man to man, Matt, who cares about language barriers, right? I don't use much language with my wife. So what if Helen's ex can't speak Spanish? You don't know how lucky you are, man, living on your own. What I wouldn't give ..."

"Tell you what, Bobby," I said, "you try living alone for five years—no, make it five months—and then we'll check in about how lucky you are."

"Yeah, well, I'm just saying."

Helen began to sob. Caroline looked horrified. Her son looked embarrassed. Gabriela put her arm around our distraught neighbor, and Helen's son took a bandana from his pocket and gave it to his mother as a handkerchief. If I could have cast a spell on everyone—stunned them into silence, then had them all stand on my rug to be magically transported back to their respective homes with no memory of this potluck—I would have been already chanting.

Gabriela squeezed Helen's hand and offered an apology for her thoughtlessness. "Sorry, Helen. Sometimes I get infected."

We all pretended that we understood what Gabby was trying to say. We focused on the *Sorry*.

I tried to think about Helen's annual winter trips to Hawaii and how much money she probably had in her retirement account to alleviate how badly I was feeling for this woman sobbing at my dinner table, but the images of palm trees and stock balances wouldn't free me from this trap.

Somebody say something, please.

"I've never kissed anyone." Caroline's kid broke the silence with his confession. "Just thinking about it scares me."

His young-boy-honesty shocked me. *My* first kiss I knew I'd done it right, but I could also tell that it would've been a better kiss if I were kissing the girl I wanted to kiss and not the girl in front of me, who was stand-in until I could snag the girl I really wanted. This was not something I felt I could blurt out at a potluck dinner with three adult women.

"What if you do it wrong?" The kid was on a roll. "The person you're kissing wouldn't tell you, right? She'd just pretend it was good, so it wouldn't hurt your feelings."

The teen's meditation on kissing tipped the moment over the edge. Helen's body began to shake with the loss of the only person she'd ever had sex with. I'm not psychic. I know this because in a moment of weakness the poor woman had told a neighbor-slash-friend, who then let it slip in one of those "don't tell anybody" conversations, and soon after it was coming out of Postmaster Bobby's mouth. The asshole divulged this excruciatingly personal information to anyone who was willing to listen when they came in to buy stamps.

The intensity of Helen's breakdown in my livingroom impelled Caroline into action. She edged Gabby aside and swooped over Helen.

"We've all been there, haven't we?" She looked at Gabby and me for confirmation. In her best sympathetic voice, Gabby said, "Oh, yes, yes," as she waved a hand in front of her face as if she were shooing away an invisible past lover. Then she moved the knife that was pointing at Helen's heart. "I have been there. Sure."

After that, it was my turn to agree, so I nodded my solidarity. *Lord, let this be quick!* There was no way in hell that I was going to tell this table of strangers—grown women and teenage boys—about paying for my ex's abortion—a pregnancy that was the result of her infidelity. Never.

Why wasn't silence The Great Healer?

"You take your time, Helen." Caroline kept talking. "You've done nothing wrong."

I understood now why she had worn coveralls; she was the kind of woman who was always at the ready to dive into whatever work was needed, even if it was emotional. She unclenched Helen's fist and stuffed another tissue in it.

Instead of feeling totally grateful for Caroline's words, there was a part of me that was also irritated. I was thinking: Really, Helen? Have you done nothing wrong? Is that possible? Not every left woman is completely innocent. Maybe Helen got drunk every night? Maybe her ex was tired of picking up her empty wine glasses? Maybe some of our sympathy should be with her husband? Maybe he was leaving an American drunk to hook up with a Spanish drunk—a woman who came with her own vineyard? Alright, telling Helen "to take her time" was commendable, but the rest of what had gone on in the privacy of Helen's home we could only guess at. When my neighbors saw my ex packing, what could they have known about the reason for her leaving? She certainly wasn't going to 'fess up to what she'd one. And I wasn't going to tell anyone.

I imagined that my neighbors probably thought *I* was The Bad Guy.

I'd had enough. This potluck was so much more than I'd signed up for. I just wanted these women to go.

"Pumpkin pie," I said. "Anyone?"

Silence.

Okay, so my attempt to change the subject with pie was horrific. It just made us all more aware of our discomfort. Let me say again: this pot-fucking-luck wasn't my idea. Why should I be made to feel like an idiot in my own home? Talking, talking—what good was it doing? I wanted to say, Enjoy your pie. Have another slice. Isn't pie-eating a better use for your mouths?

I was raised in a home which kept communication to a minimum, and that was more than okay with me. I didn't want my mom or my dad to sit me down to tell me what had put them in their bad mood, or to explain the workings of their hearts and minds. Other people's parents were Talking Things Through all the way to divorce courts. My parents just got on with The Job of Living. And most of their living was about going to work, with the occasional night out. I don't know if they came home from their rare nights out having had heart-to-hearts; all I knew was that they kept us housed, fed, and generally cared for. The absence of family meetings spared us all. Even on her deathbed, my mother kept to herself. Instead of using her final moments to push out some last-minute words, she squeezed my hand. *I love you*, it said, and *Goodbye*. One touch. Four words.

Oh, Mr. Franklin, it is not only disposable income that is new. It is also the need to speak what we feel before an audience of millions on TV, or at a relative stranger's dining table.

Having bonded with a little handholding, the two divorcées eventually left at the same time. Born again as confidantes. Their connection was palpable—each had entered my home with a surrogate husband, and each was leaving with a brand new BFF.

As Gabby and I stood watching them walk off in the dark, I noticed that the candle inside the pumpkin had burned down. Without a flame inside, it just looked like an ugly doorstop.

The relief that washed over me at my home's sudden emptiness was replaced by something unexpected—the privilege of having someone I loved standing beside me. From this distance, I had sympathy for their losses. How replaceable they must have felt. This surge of understanding for the divorcées made me want more time with Gabby, not less. Plus, when you think about it, having separate homes is not really that frugal.

After dinner guests leave, a home looks like the aftermath of a massacre rather than the remnants of a gathering to Break Bread. And this aftermath was no different. Knives stuck out at various angles. Chicken bones waited for the worms. I put the leftover pie in the refrigerator and called dibs on the last slice for tomorrow's breakfast, but Gabby didn't hear me. She'd already retreated to her private island.

My neighbors' departure made my house feel even more silent than usual. I didn't want to dissect the evening and I was hoping that Gabby would feel the same. We cleared the mess, walking back and forwards from table to sink with an unspoken and easy negotiation. She turned on her music and we were both transported. For her, it was Nicaragua. For me, it was the heart-to-heart I wanted to have before we sat down and got lost in TV.

In my head I began to practice bits of what I wanted to say. I wanted to do it right. To say it simply. I wanted her to hear me. I wanted to be understood.

"Do you want to get married and have a baby?" I blurted. "Now? Before it's too late?" (So much for practicing.)

What can I say? Gabby understands me well enough to know I'm clumsy with words. Past experience has taught me that even when I try to phrase things right, I get it wrong. So far, she has not held this against me.

"How do you know that I'm not already married?"

This was not the reply I'd been anticipating. I'd not given her past much thought in terms of romance. When I thought about Gabby in Nicaragua, I always thought about political stuff. Never about love. She could've been married.

"And how do you know I'm not already a mama?"

We talked so little about her past. I knew there was a lot she wanted to forget and I wanted her to start her life afresh, without resurrecting bad memories. I wanted for her what she wanted for herself, so I did not pry. But now that I had posed my questions and gotten this response, I was curious. By wanting to respect what she wanted to forget, there was much I didn't know. She could have had three children, for all I knew. If she'd been a teenage mom, she could've even been a grandmother . . .

"Well? Are you married? Do you have children?"

I saw the hesitation on her face, but then she surrendered. "I once was married. But it finish. After they take my little girl."

I felt as if my feet were falling through the floorboards. My mouth was frozen. I had respected her decision to let her past remain in the past, but this new information was drastic. Her silence about her child felt like a betrayal. How could she have not told me something as important as having a child taken?

She offered me more information without my asking. "When they took my baby, I went to bed for one year. I never know who take my little girl. I never know why they take her. Maybe because of my brother? Because of politics? My husband he could not look at me in bed. He could not look at my brother. After ten month he leave. No more daughter. No more husband. Nothing. So I leave. To America."

I didn't know if I should ask more questions. I normally left the decision to stop talking about her past up to her. But this time I felt uncertain.

"What was her name?"

"Paola. Paola Iris Mendoza."

It is difficult to distinguish between the silence of shock and the silence of wisdom. This was not a time to think about what I wanted. Her revelation made me aware of how much I had been responsible for the shape of our relationship. I felt like an asshole. Going on about frugality, economy of words, when all along Gabby had me beat. This was silence as The Great Healer.

Because we don't share a home, I still have nights when I am alone in my bed. On these nights, about fifty percent of the time, I can't fall asleep. Worry about money keeps me awake. I think things like, will I have to work until I drop dead simply to keep up with my rent? Will there ever come a time when I will be able to afford a vacation? I don't mean a long weekend, but two whole weeks with no work. There are nights when my worry works me up into such a state that it spills out and I shock myself by crying. Actual sobs. I've been able to keep these sobbing nights from Gabriela. I admit that my nighttime panic attacks have played a large part in my advocating for us living separately. But now, so what? What she has kept from me is so much more than the discovery of my midnight sobbing.

So. Power? Control? I had no idea I had any. But I guess I have called most of the shots in our relationship. I didn't mean to bulldoze over Gabby's feelings. I didn't mean to make demands without asking her what she wanted. I wasn't trying to lord it over her. I've just been too fixated on myself. But Gabby's past makes my worries pale in comparison.

"I don't want to talk more now. We talk tomorrow. Okay?"

"Sure, Gabs. Tomorrow." I hit the *pause* button in my mind.

Gabby hit *play* on the remote. This time we watched an English police drama. It was about someone who impersonated rich people. The criminal joined an elite golf club, made his way into the locker room, took all the car keys he could find, then drove away with the most expensive car in the parking lot, which had the added bonus of the owner's wallet inside a jacket lying on the backseat. The point was that rich people trust golf-club parking lots because they feel they are with their own kind. They leave things in their cars that they would never leave in parking lots used by the non-rich.

One golf-club member says to the policeman, "My God, if your valuables are not safe at a golf club, then what is the world coming to?"

"Quite," responds the policeman, whose electricity has just been cut because all his money went to a mortgage payment and child support.

Gabby hit *mute*. "We talk so little bit. And my life in Nicaragua is so big. I think is better to say nothing. Silent is help. But I keep Paola inside me. She is everywhere with me. I play her some music. I dance for her. Then I come back to you." Gabby kept her finger on the mute button. "You ask if I want to be married because you want this? Or you ask because you think I want this?"

"I don't know what I want, Gabs. I was hoping you knew what you wanted and I would go along with it. If I'm squandering my life, I don't want to squander your life too."

"*Squander?*"

"It means to throw something away without thinking about it. I don't want to throw your life away."

She released the *mute* button, but I could see her still thinking about *squander*. It was as if I were watching her through my binoculars; she was having a conversation with herself. I didn't want to interrupt. I found my own thing to think about: What was I doing to make her life better?

America is Gabby's second chance; to begin her life again. Now that I know how huge her beginning is, I don't want to stand in her way. Plus, when it comes right down to it, I believe in love above all else—above industry, above frugality. And since I believe this, then what better way is there to live than to join her in this loving?

On his way to solve the crime, the policeman stops to pay his utility bill. This prompts me to get up to turn off the light. From the livingroom window, I watch as Helen's son brings in their dog and turns off the porch light. At Caroline's house, a mystery car has arrived. A man I don't recognize gets out.

Gabby has lost interest in the TV. "You want to go to bed?"

"Yes, Gabs. Give me a sec. I'll be right with you."

I kill the TV and make my way up to join her. From the staircase window, I see Caroline's house is dark, but at Helen's, the bedroom light is still on.

The Evolution of Beauty

I didn't think of it as I stood at the supermarket checkout to buy the glittery red plastic food container. I still didn't think of it when I spooned the cornbread and sausage mixture into the glitzy Tupperware designed especially for the holidays. But today, as I was making the mushroom sauce, the thought began to creep in. As I removed the cabbage from the boiling water, as I peeled each leaf from its core, the thought began to grow. As I removed yesterday's mixture from the refrigerator, I could not push the thought away. As I spooned the filling into the first leaf, then rolled it into a small parcel, tucked in its edges, the thought was there. As I placed each cabbage parcel into the dish, packing each one as close to the next as possible, I thought: I hope they do not come apart.

*

When the stripper arrived at the lesbian "bachelor" party, I felt like I was in one of those dreams where someone opens the bathroom door and catches you peeing. The only straight party guest had ordered her for "entertainment," but mimicking straight men was not the way forward for this night of prenuptial fun. We were not prudes, but the heavy makeup and the long painted nails on the stripper made it clear she was not for us. We tried to be extra polite, pretending we were amused, but her entrance made our own bodies clench in response.

As the stripper took off her coat and hat, she apologized for her lateness, explaining that her babysitter had not shown up. She set up her music, standing with her back to us in a red glittery bikini and high-heeled shoes. I tried not to look at her, but I couldn't help myself; she was the spitting image of a younger version of my mother, which made me want to cover her back up.

The explanation for her late arrival made us unclench a little, and we invited her to join The Circle of the Fully Clothed. One of the party guests poured her a Scotch. I fought the urge to call her by my mother's name. The rest of the women tried to make her feel welcome by beginning a conversation about childcare.

I was grateful that she was being invited to sit instead of perform, but even with this new feeling of gratitude, the half-clothed woman juxtaposed with the fully-clothed women made it difficult for me to adjust. Plus, glitter has always made me suspicious—what is it supposed to hide? Add? Was the sparkle supposed to improve her appeal? This woman did not need glitter to enhance her appearance. She was beautiful. Even more beautiful, I suspected, had she shown up to work without the mask of heavy makeup.

As the other women leaned into the conversation, and as the ones who were mothers exchanged tips on where to look for childcare providers, I studied her attractiveness, questioning the theory that our choice of mate is based on the survival of our species. Was this stripper beautiful to help her escape a predator or to sneak up on her prey? Neither choice seemed to fit.

Other than her beauty, I also noticed that her face could have originated from a mix of ethnicities, and that she spoke in an accent that was not North American. This added an extra feeling of kinship with her that none of the other party guests shared—she and I were the only two women in the room not raised in the U.S.

Her accent had a distinctly South American lilt. One of the brides-to-be asked, "Are you from Brazil?"

"No," she said, "I am from another South American country. Beginning with B. Next to Brazil. A country no one in this America remembers. Why you don't guess?"

Instead of watching her remove her clothes, the entertainment became Guess The Stripper's Country of Origin. After a couple of guesses, there was a short silence. Then the other bride-to-be said: "We give up!"

"Bolivia!" said the entertainer.

"Oh," said the doctor.

"Bolivia!" said the lawyer. "Who'd've thunk it?"

The betrothed couple could relate to the stripper's babysitter woes; they already had three children. Their upcoming nuptials, though much desired, came in at a distant second to their love for children. To attend the party, they had left their two girls and a boy in the care of a woman who was also from South America. The couple offered the Bolivian woman the names of two highly recommended, trustworthy sitters who had cared for their children in the past.

The other women in the room who were not yet mothers, but who were in the midst of planning their own pregnancies—as well as the one who was already six months along—were also interested to hear of the stripper's problems with childcare and the difficulty of finding sitters in the evening when one's work is irregular and often last-minute.

In addition to the doctor and the lawyer, there was a professor, a visual artist, and a business executive at the party. It was unlikely that any of them, after the birth of their child, would have to run out at the last minute to remove their clothes to pay off a bill. Still, they felt bound to one another by motherhood—current or prospective.

"Take the night off," the doctor prescribed.

"Yes, take the night off," the others chorused.

They sent the entertainer home early with the phone numbers of possible sitters tucked into the pocket of her un-glittery jeans.

When she left, the women continued with talk of pregnancy—who was already trying, who'd had miscarriages, things to look for in a sperm donor, or from a sperm bank, and what to ask a prospective babysitter who is interviewing for the job of caring for a two-mothered child.

*

I was raised among mothers who did not have to look for sitters; instead, these women worked from sewing-machines in the corners of their livingrooms, close to their kitchens, so that they could jump up easily to check whatever was on the stove. My mother was one of these women. And like the

Bolivian stripper, her beauty did not help her to escape a predator or to sneak up on her prey. Instead, she managed her life by becoming the dominatrix of her own time: Saturdays she cleaned the home; Sundays she cooked for the week; Thursday afternoons she shopped and paid bills. The rest of her time she spent at the machine in the livingroom. She even kept an empty milk bottle by the foot-pedal to use instead of wasting time by going upstairs to the cold bathroom on the unheated top floor. And every three evenings a week, the factory owner came by to drop off a bundle of dress parts, to pick up the dresses she had already made whole, and to eat a plate of whatever was on her stove.

"It's black-eyed peas tonight. You still want a plate?"

Even to this humblest of meals, her boss did not say no. He never said no. He always looked as if he were ready for more food, and to do what he could to stay in our home a few minutes longer—to stare at my mother, as her eyes darted from one livingroom ornament to another, careful never to meet his gaze.

Once he'd emptied his plate, he gave my mother the next set of instructions: "I want you to sew these dresses the same way as the previous bundle—stitch the seams as close to the edge as you can. We've cut these ones tight. Smaller. To make cabbage."

The dresses beyond the number required of the docket— the extras that you can squeeze out if you make the seams tighter—are called "cabbage." Cabbage sells at ninety percent profit—all of which goes to the boss, none to the seamstresses.

Though none of these women had to pull apart furniture to throw chair legs into the fire to heat their homes, and though none of the mothers I knew were working as adult entertainers to pay their bills, it was still difficult for them to feed their families. To help with this problem, they made an unspoken pact, never to allow the number of children they had to exceed three. There was no talk about rights. No angst about when life begins. Just one question: *Can we afford another child?*

While my mother was not a predator, she was practical; her marriage was for her protection; her children's christenings were their protection. She hung a blue talisman around her neck to ward off the Evil Eye, and she pinned smaller versions of this protective pendant under the collars of my baby clothes. Her rituals were not about the reward of an afterlife, but the guarantee of a place in a community that would not let her drown if she kept swimming in the same direction as all of the other women. If she did not go off to explore her own life, then she would always have meat to add to the cabbage boiling on her stove.

I came home from school one day to find my mother covered in strands of red thread, with bias-binding hanging out of her mouth. Sleeves and collars and fronts and backs that she had already sewn together and trimmed in sequins were strewn about—hanging on a chair, at her feet, all around the base of the sewing machine. Party clothes. Glittery dresses. Identical. In multiples. Lying limp. She looked like she'd been caught in the unglamorous moment when everyone has left the party, when the glasses are empty except for the dregs, when the ashtrays are full, and the dirty napkins have yet to find their way to the trash.

*

There was nothing trashy about the stripper. Because of how much skin her red glittery bikini revealed, I could see her body relax as she was invited to join the group. The more natural the conversation became, the less she struggled to find the right words. Still, I could sense how tiring it was for her to speak in a language in which she was not yet fluent. First, she had to think of the sentence. Then, she had to check to see if she had all the vocabulary. Then, she had to check to see if the words were in the right order. On her face, I saw the hope that figuring this out had not taken her too long. Finally, she said, "My son is three year old. His dad left us one year ago. I start dancing three months after he go. I know he not come back."

The doctor poured her another Scotch.

Though speaking in a language that was not her own was tiring, it did not exhaust her as much the three hours she had spent cleaning houses, followed by the one hour traveling by subway to the bachelor party, then the hour she had budgeted to dance while taking off her clothes, and the final hour of work that night to travel back to her child.

*

Counting the hours women work is something I have done since I left home. I add these hours as obsessively as other women tally their caloric intake: I have tallied the hours the seamstresses I grew up with spent sewing for factories; and I have tallied the hours that the women I know stand on their feet cutting hair or stacking supermarket shelves. I have tried to count the work hours of the women I know who clean the bathrooms in offices, in schools, and in post offices. My list of women's work hours goes on and on. In my tallies, I note that most do not get maternity leave, and most do not have retirement plans, and few have paid vacation days. Numbers and charts and tables scroll through my dreams. There are mornings when I wake up counting.

My counting obsession kicked in again as soon as the stripper took off her high-heeled shoes and curled her feet under her on the bachelor-party-bed. At the time, I felt that the party guests should have left the room so that she could seize the opportunity to let her body relax and to catch up on sleep. But since I am not a mother myself, it had not occurred to me that she could not sleep through the night—even if the room was given to her as a gift—knowing that her sitter had to leave as soon as the hours of childcare she'd paid for had run out. Instead she went home early, fully paid for the entertainment she'd been liberated from having to provide. Plus, the energy that she had saved by not having to strip was likely sizable. But it was not something I could measure or count. It is not as easy to tally up the lives of mothers who strip as it is for mothers who sew. Unlike X-ray machines that can document the deterioration of a spine after thirty years of bending over to push the material under a sewing-machine's foot, there is no medical equipment that can record how much of the heart's fabric deteriorates after years of being paid to strip.

*

While the stuffed cabbage cooked, I turned my attention to what needed to be cleared up. I threw away the torn outer layers of the cabbage as well as its tough core. Then I stacked what needed to be washed, which included the empty Tupperware container. Because the red plastic was dirty, its glitter had dulled, though this did not affect how well it sealed. When the dishes were done, I opened the oven to check on the leafy parcels, knowing that their beauty depended on how well they held what was inside.

GOD IS MERCIFUL

Two policemen came to our door and told my husband that something was wrong with his vehicle registration and he had to go with them to the station. "Five minutes, madam." They looked me in the eye. Smiled. Promised. "One cup of coffee, madam, and we will bring him back. We will escort him ourselves. Personally."

They took my husband. I made a cup of coffee. Then I made another. Ten minutes passed. Ten months. Ten years.

Twelve years after they took him, as I was about to feed my cow, I opened my door and there he was, lying in the dirt. Missing thumbs. Missing an eye. No breath. I cried for so long that my body was so full of loss there was no room for food. Rage filled me with the desire to go to the police station with my kitchen knife hidden beneath my clothes, to stab two policemen—any policemen—the first two I saw. But even in this rage and grief, I knew I could never kill, even to avenge my husband's death. I could not kill for many reasons—because I could not imagine taking another life, because I could not imagine getting away with it—but the biggest reason was that if I were caught then who would take care of my children?

Four months after they took my husband, I gave birth. Twins. Boys! A pride that filled me with love, then emptied me with the anticipation of what their lives might become. If their father could be taken from me so easily, then why would I not anticipate the same destiny for my sons?

I used to have so many questions. And I waited—stupidly—as if there would come a day when my questions would be answered. But now I see so much wider, farther. And I know so much more than before: my old questions were never going to be answered, even if I had believed that I had a personal relationship with God.

Those of you who do not believe in a redeemer, hang onto your conviction. I'm dead and I still do not know if God exists. I am simply suspended in this place of all-seeing, but not all-knowing.

Just before my death I saw my own country's flag and my own country's army, coming towards my village to bulldoze our homes. When the soldiers were close enough that I could see their guns, I knew that I had to abandon the place in which I had lived since my wedding; my own two rooms—my kitchen and another room, the one in which we ate, watched the news, and slept. As the flags and tanks got closer, I knew that I had to abandon not only my home, my sky, my soil, but also my cow.

The question I now hold is this: Was it more important to protect an animal or to protect my own body?

Run, Kholood, I told myself. If I chose to stay, destruction was certain. If I left, there was a possible future. So as soon as it was dark, I took my two boys' hands and we ran.

We had gone less than a mile before I said to my sister-in-law, "Take them. Please. I have to go back for my cow."

Once your life is taken from you, there is no looking forward, only memories to question: Why return for my cow? Would she have run with me? Could she have run faster than the bulldozers? Could we have run faster than the bullets? Could I have used her as a shield? If I had managed to rescue her to keep my boys fed for a year or so, would her slaughter have come on the day of my own choosing? In a safe place, far from my home? Which was never truly safe, now that I'm speaking honestly.

War or no war, no place is safe at any time for any woman, even if she has a husband; that husband will always be stronger than she is. Even if he never imagines hurting her, she will do the imagining for him.

Peaceful sleep? Does a woman ever know it? No woman I have eaten breakfast with has looked like she's had one night of restful sleep since her monthly bleeding began. The world is not the same place for men and women. Never. Anywhere.

In my living, not one week passed when I didn't look at my kitchen knives and wonder if that day would be the day that one of my knives would be used against me by my husband or my father or a solider or a stranger—or any man who sees a woman alone and seizes his chance to have dominion over her.

And yet, it turned out that it was not I who had to watch out for a man who wanted dominion over another's life, but my husband. When my brother-in-law helped me to bring in my husband's body, we saw the marks where they'd hung him from meat hooks—his ripped skin testimony to the violence of men.

For years I listened to the men in my family sitting in my home drinking the coffee I had made for them, talking about the fight for democracy. Democracy? Let me tell you about the fight for it. It is difficult to keep your mind on this fight when your first thought is how you will feed your children. I was not an ignorant woman. I had a father who valued his daughters as much as his sons—our educations were the same. I was schooled. I read newspapers. As the men drank my coffee, I sat in the kitchen listening to the same news that they were listening to, and this is what I learned: there are no immediate Happily Ever Afters following a country's revolution. What follow are arguments, turmoil, and empty food shelves. I could not add to this with the violence of hunger.

The two other mothers who ran from my village with me had left behind their teenage sons. "Some sacrifices," one said, "are stronger than a mother's love for her children." They left their boys to stand in the line of fire. "We do this," the other said, as if I didn't already know, "in the name of victory."

The first mother to speak was my neighbor. Her house had been so close to mine that I could hear her husband shouting at her, "Bring me my food! Don't sit there like a cow waiting for rain."

In life, I used to pepper my sentences with *Thanks be to God* and *God is merciful*. But now I ask: How did God show me his mercy? Even in this moment, I still have no evidence of it; only this hole in my forehead, this gunshot wound to remind me of my mistake—going back for my cow.

The Fall

The problem became real the day after New York State announced to the world that it was now legal within its borders for two people of the same sex to marry. Even when you reject most of the expectations of a culture, some things come into your mind, involuntarily, that have no business being there, like the opening bars to Wagner's Bridal Chorus: *Dum, dum, de-dum.*

When Neelam heard the news she was alone in the apartment mopping the kitchen floor. She turned up the volume on the radio and pretended the scraggly mop in her hand was a bride she was accompanying down the kitchen aisle, between the countertops and the stove, as she sang *dum, dum, de-dum* to the dry words about lawmakers, the marriage bill, and the thirty-three to twenty-nine vote. Then Michelle walked in and caught her. In her embarrassment, Neelam felt the *b* to the end of each word—*dumb, dumb, de dumb* . . . "I know. I got carried away. But it's great news, right?"

Because Michelle and Neelam are of the same sex, and because they live in New York, the news was not only a public announcement, but also an intimate message that held a subtext that could have a profound impact on their lives. If the public text was *Same sex couples can now marry*, then their private subtext was *Now what?*

Subtext was a word that loomed large in their lives. In Michelle's discussions with her English Lit students, subtext was often the focus. Perched on top of her desk, in a tailored suit, her dreads perfectly twisted, she'd ask the thirty or so distracted faces, "What do you think is going on in this scene?"

She was not oblivious to the fact that most of her students did not have the time to contemplate subtexts. She had once lived the same life. But in the time it had taken to go from junior faculty to assistant professor, she had gradually forgotten how difficult it was to contemplate the subtexts of books when life consisted of running from home to work to school to home. She was still aware, though, that most of the students who fell asleep in her class did so because they had come straight from their nightshifts, and not because they had spent the night drinking away their student loans.

Her friend who taught at an upscale college in New Jersey told her of a recent craze among his students—attending class in pajamas. For these pajamas-to-class students, this was supposed to amount to some kind of protest. "I know I'm supposed to know what their protest is about," he said, "but, honestly, I don't care enough to ask. And so far, no one has volunteered to tell me." He had done the impossible—landed a full-time tenure-track job just months after defending his dissertation—but his elation quickly dissipated once he faced the demands of a classroom full of young people whose identities as students seemed to hang like albatrosses around their necks.

"Oh, please," Michelle rolled her eyes. "Forget pajamas. *My* students come to work in uniforms—nurses' aides, eldercare attendants, security guards. They've got no time for pajama protests." She was not paid as much as her upscale-college-professor friend, but at least she didn't have an existential crisis each time Spring Break rolled around. While his students flew off to spend the week at a ski resort or a beach, he remained home, obsessively checking his bank balance to make sure he had enough to pay the next installments of his car note and student loans.

"There's not much protesting—real or fake—at my job," said Michelle. Once the subject of teaching came up, she was on a roll. "The students are there because they *need* that degree and they can get it at a good price. My problem is helping them to find the time to study when they're full-time students and full-time workers. *And* parents. I say to them, 'I know most of you chose this class because it fits into your schedule and because it is required, but since we're all going to be here twice a week for sixteen weeks, lets promise ourselves that we'll make time to think about what we read, okay?' This week we're reading *A Portrait of the Artist as a Young Man*. I asked them to think about it for at least one subway trip."

The majority of Michelle's students were women between their late twenties and late forties. For them, talking about subtext did not feel as urgent as sleeping—or even daydreaming—so they often dozed or drifted, which meant that most of her teaching involved reining their minds back into the room and back to the page. For the Joyce discussion, she pleaded, "Come on, people, did you even read this chapter? Surely you have something you want to say about Stephen

Daedalus in this scene?" With no response to her question, she continued to hold forth on a fictionalized version of the writer's early life, wondering what she could find in the subtext that might speak to these breadwinning women, most of them children of immigrants, many of them already mothers. Were any of them listening? Did any of them even care about deconstructing guilt, Catholicism, and the politics of a tiny country they might never have the desire to visit?

As Michelle led discussions on the texts and subtexts of a variety of 20th Century books, Neelam was still working—illegally. Working "off the books" was all about what happened on the lines, not between the lines. When Neelam's boss asked her to do something, she did it; she didn't have the time to contemplate the subtext of Raquel's request for a protein shake at precisely noon each day.

Raquel took the shake from Neelam as if the future of the world depended on its noonday consumption. "I thank God," she pronounced to the imaginary audience she always carried around in her head, "I live in a country where I can get blueberries all year round."

After a handful of giant gulps, lunch was over. Neelam took the empty glass from her boss and immediately rinsed it.

Raquel handed Neelam a slip of paper. "Here's the list of what I need done."

Neelam glanced down at the enormity of the projects. Her hands trembled in response. Raquel swung a heavily studded leather jacket about her shoulders, then added, "For the construction of the indoor pond, just call up the same people who built the solarium. Cool?"

Neelam tried her best to keep her hands still, but her anxiety had almost turned the to-do list into a fan. "What about the waterlilies?"

"I'm not sure. Call up the Botanical Garden maybe? Brooklyn? The Bronx? Whatever you think. I trust your judgment. I'll be in the studio the rest of the day, if you need me."

The door to the penthouse slammed shut. Neelam was swallowed by the silent burden of planning a celebrity wedding. Armed with a yellow highlighter and a pen, she picked up the phone and began calling construction companies and botanical gardens.

As an "illegal alien" it didn't matter what Neelam's previous education qualified her for; her ability to live and work freely boiled down to one thing—citizenship. Back in Kerala, she was qualified and already practicing midwifery. It was an understatement to say that she missed coaxing babies out of their mothers' wombs and into the world. Wiping away the placenta to reveal a tender new life was an ecstasy that she relived with each birth. From an early age midwifery was what she wanted to do with her life, and she yearned to return to it.

In the meantime, she'd made the sacrifice of moving countries to look for a way to live her life more fully. She didn't want to hide her love, and the U.S. offered her this possibility. So she had boarded the flight out of COK International Airport in Kerala, transferred in Frankfurt, and descended into JFK International in Queens, which was approximately twelve miles from lower Manhattan, where she now alighted from a subway car each day for work. For this temporary partial freedom, she'd stopped cutting umbilical cords. First, she worked as a nanny for two straight gynecologists, then as a nanny for the CEO of a company that manufactured upscale lingerie and his stay-at-home husband. Then she worked as a receptionist for a queer feminist pornographer. Presently, she was the personal assistant for an internationally known, crossover lesbian singer.

Raquel was Mistress as well as Master of the contemporary pan-sexual ballad (no pronouns, no identifying gestures of gender), whose latest CD was in every queer and straight household from New York City to Timbuktu. As soon as she heard the news about New York's same-sex marriage laws, she called Neelam. "Let's plan this wedding, girl! I'm gonna proclaim my love to the world!"

Because Raquel was a paid-up member of the U.S. mega-rich club, naturally her food and fitness routines were both planned to the last detail. She followed a macrobiotic diet and had a personal chef who made sure that her daily intake of the freshest organic ingredients was consciously cooked and artfully presented on black plates handpainted with cherry blossom designs. Words like *coulis, confits, shaved,* and *infused* were used to describe the little islands of food she consumed.

She treated her chef like a lover, always looking for an excuse to kiss him. "Thank you, Hiroki. Kiss, kiss." Her artificially femme air kisses were absurd on a five-foot-eleven-inch contralto. She prided…. No, not *prided*—she *competed* with other women for top-spot butchness. But if her competitors could have seen how she behaved around Hiroki, they would have laughed her out of the competition. Her femme moments were kept in check in public, though, and she made sure that her peroxide-white-blonde hair was kept cropped and spiked. Because of this public persona, Neelam didn't need to ask her boss if she was going to wear a suit or a dress for The Blessed Event.

"A *white* suit, Neelam. We need to get the tailor round here. Get me measured. I want it made from raw silk and the inside lined with satin. I want it to feel as good on the inside as it looks on the outside."

Before New York State made its announcement to the world, Michelle and Neelam had talked about getting married in a way that made it feel as if it were something that could happen in another life. These conversations didn't seem odd to Neelam; she grew up being taught about future lifecycles and how they would be better than the cycle she was currently living. Still, she was disappointed; she'd hoped for something different in NYC. In the first year of their relationship, while she was going through an intense bout of homesickness, she blurted, "New York or Kerala, heaven or reincarnation, they all promise the same thing—*future* happiness." It had taken months for this little outburst to build up, but as soon as her words were out, the tension left her body. She felt deflated, as well as embarrassed by the emotion she'd exhibited. She picked up *Loving Her*, and hid her mortification in the novel's open pages.

"We have a long way to go, I know," Michelle agreed. "But don't let it get you down. If you do, they win. We can create our own ceremony. We don't need to wait for the law's permission."

At the time, Michelle was big on self-creation. She had been thinking of a name change and had a list of Yoruba possibilities, but she couldn't make up her mind which one to choose. The names she liked were either too predictable like *Ife* (Love) or too off-putting like *Ige* (breech birth). She wanted something in the middle, something believable and suitable, something like *Bejide* (born during the rainy season) because she was in fact born in New York in April. But whenever it came to making a final decision, she couldn't do it. Tossing aside a name that belonged to a former oppressor—in favor of a name from an ethnic group to whom her ancestral connection was uncertain—seemed too arbitrary. Whatever name she chose would be nothing more than an intelligent guess; she could have just as easily been the descendant of the Hausa or the Igbo. She could have even been the great, great, great, great granddaughter of the Akan.

"I don't want to invent our own ceremony." The whine in her own voice caught Neelam by surprise.

"Okay, Nee. Agreed. We'll wait till the law courts catch up."

They both turned over the pages in their respective novels and allowed the words to embrace them.

For a while, Neelam had kept a sari not exactly hidden but tucked away in the back of her closet. This sari was not The Sari she wanted to wear if and when she got married, but it was a similar sari to her Dream Sari. She had bought this version with the fantasy that she might one day give it to a seamstress and say: I want my wedding dress to be like this, but I want it to be turquoise. And I want the *choli* to have three-quarter sleeves, with golden embroidery around the neck. Just a little. Not too much.

Though she had all this planned, she never went as far as imagining herself wearing this wedding sari. But now that the New York lawmakers had caught up with her, she could allow herself to make the Dream Sari real. No more waiting for future happiness—here was the possibility of *present* joy. Once she and Michelle decided on a date for their nuptials, the wedding sari would be made and worn. And a little while after the Justice of the Peace made her pronouncement, Neelam would be granted a new identity—*Wife*. And who knows, maybe a year or so later, after midwifery school, she could add a couple more identities—no more Illegal Alien Indian Lover; instead, Legal American Midwife and Wife.

Michelle hadn't noticed a significant difference in her life since she had changed her identity from full-time doctoral student to full-time professor. Her apartment hadn't suddenly sprouted another bedroom or acquired an office. Her desk was still stuck in the corner of the bedroom. Her furniture hadn't suddenly gotten sturdier. She still sat on a futon instead of a couch. She still ate a bagel with cream cheese each morning because it could be bought from the van right in front of the college and could keep her full until her classes were taught and her office hours were finished.

"Toasted bagel with—"

"Cream cheese." The street vendor finished her sentence. "You are like a clock. When I see you I know it is 7:30 A.M."

Great! This was her dream come true, to be a street vendor's timekeeper. "Am I that predictable?" The vendor raised an eyebrow in response, then slathered enough cream cheese on her bagel to feed a family of four. He handed it to her in a greaseproof bag, but the cream cheese proved victorious, oozing out of the opening. "Have the bagel for lunch, instead," he offered. "That will be different."

"This *is* my lunch—breakfast *and* lunch." Tomorrow, she thought, I'll try the juice bar down the street. Adding a scoop of hemp powder to keep her full would probably knock the price up to six bucks. Six bucks for a shake! (Maybe when she got tenure.)

The doctoral research was over. The dissertation was written and defended. She had the letters PhD after her name, and like her New Jersey friend, she'd even landed a full-time, tenure-track job in a record amount of time on the market. In place of all her graduate work, she now had two Comp classes in addition to two Twentieth Century Lit classes. On difficult days, her four/four load—a total of one hundred and twenty students each week, each semester—gave her heart palpitations. She required all one hundred and twenty of her students to attend office hours (at least once) and to write multiple papers because she could not bring herself to reduce novels to multiple-choice questions like:

In which book do you find the character of Janie Crawford?

1. *Cane* (Jean Toomer)
2. *Their Eyes Were Watching God* (Zora Neale Hurston)
3. *A Portrait of the Artist As a Young Man* (James Joyce)

As for the doctoral mirage of Summers Off, she had yet to stumble upon it as she wandered the desert of her so-called professorial life. She taught summer school because her rent and student loans required it. Her spring semester had only just finished; now she had to send in her summer course descriptions. She'd already typed them out, but could not bring herself to press *Send*. Instead, she sat back in her bedroom/office chair, looking dejected. "I feel like I'm going to be paying off this ninety grand for the rest of my life. I can't imagine us ever having the money for a deposit on our own home. Some days I find myself wishing my job was in Detroit or Pittsburgh. At least that way we'd stand a chance of saving for a deposit. Neither of us have family that can help ..." She didn't go as far as accusing Neelam directly for the part she played in not being able to climb out of their financial rut, but now that the words were out of her mouth, they hung in midair like fog. Since grad school, she'd watched friends, with parental help or a wealthier spouse, putting deposits on apartments. "It's a struggle, Nee, to remember how lucky I am. Promise you will kick me if I start complaining about my job in front of people who are still on the job market."

"Promise." *Perhaps I should kick you now,* Neelam thought, *for complaining in front a midwife who cannot practice midwifery; a student who is repeating a degree she has already earned, a woman who has moved backwards into workplace invisibility.* But instead of speaking her thoughts, she transformed her indignation into guilt. Truth be told, she didn't need to hear Michelle's lamentations to feel like she was holding them back as a couple. It was her guilt that pushed her to excel in her studies; if she couldn't yet become a model legal citizen, then at least she could be a model student, never missing a class, never blowing off her homework.

She walked over to the computer, sat on the floor, and looked up at Michelle. It didn't matter from what angle she looked at her, her lover always looked regal. What had she done to win this stunning prize? She took Michelle's hand from the computer mouse and kissed it. "One more year, I promise. I'll have graduated, I'll get a better job, and things will ease up." She put Michelle's hand back on the mouse. "Press *Send*. Your reward will be a summer's worth of Farmer's Market abundance transformed into delectable goodness by Yours Truly."

To get her student visa Neelam had asked a wealthy uncle to photocopy one of his bank balances and to provide an accompanying letter to vouch that he would pay her college fees. The charade did the trick. Her visa was granted, and within weeks of her entry she had landed a day job as a nanny, which allowed her to attend school at night.

Though she did not have to wear a uniform to work, she was like Michelle's students inasmuch as she had to fight not to fall asleep in class, sometimes from exhaustion, sometimes from exasperation. Her college classes were on the same level as her high school classes in Kerala, so when her intelligence wasn't insulted, her patience was being tested. While her U.S. peers were being taught how to structure an argument, she projected a public appearance of serenity, but inside she was screaming, *Come on. Let's go!*

She never allowed what was inside her to slip out—a restraint that came in handy elsewhere in NYC. She was patient in ATM and MTA lines. She didn't even get frustrated in midtown traffic on the rare occasions she took a taxi. But the one thing that made her blood boil was standing in a queue to hand over her below-minimum-wage money to the bursar to pay for an education that she already had. The two-minute exchange when she parted with her hard-earned dollars in exchange for a bursar's receipt never got easier.

Her childhood training in politeness also meant that it was not difficult for her to sit unnoticed in the classroom, but her consistent A grades guaranteed that her professors knew her name. In her Honors Colloquium, the professor, loud enough for the entire class to hear, had said, "Well done, Ms. Menon. This was a good paper! Perhaps now we will hear more from you in class?" After that, he tried to catch her eye when asking the class to respond to a question. In the discussion of *The Stranger*, the professor looked at her and asked, "Would you say, at the end of the story, Meursault has overcome society's judgment, or do you think what stands out more is that he rebelled against conformity?"

She had a lot to say about society's judgment and rebellion, but she felt uncomfortable attracting this kind of attention to herself. Instead, she held onto her invisibility with tenacity and responded to her professor's pleading glances by lowering her eyes to the desk. Keeping to herself had become second nature since her U.S. arrival. At first, she did it to keep her alien status unnoticed, but after a while it became a habit.

When Michelle's friends came over for dinner, they watched Neelam ladle soups, toss salads, make sauces, arrange circles of shrimp on their plates, and spoon cocktail sauce over each tiny curve of flesh. As they watched, she thought she saw pity on their faces. She could live with their pity because it was temporary; it would disappear once she was an equal contributing partner. But one night, when Michelle had invited over a colleague from the Anthropology department, Neelam caught something else on this dinner guest's face; something hidden, something that gave a hard-edged expression to the anthropologist's eyes.

At previous dinners, Michelle had sat at the table like another guest and thanked her, casually, for what was set before her. Don't thank me, Neelam wanted to say. Help. But even at home, the habit of her invisibility got the better of her, and so she said nothing. She was waiting for the day when her partner would see this imbalance for herself; but for the moment, with the anthropologist sitting at their dinner table, Michelle's attentiveness shifted even further away from her lover.

Michelle spooned the shrimp curry onto her colleague's plate with a care that Neelam had not felt from her lover in a while. The anthropologist leaned forward to sniff. "This smells amazing," she said, looking directly into Michelle's eyes. Neelam could feel a bubble forming around the two of them, and as the meal was consumed there was nothing she could do to enter their closed-off space.

After the evening was over, Neelam asked, "So how did you two first meet?" She winced at her own question; it was something you asked lovers.

"Women's Studies," said Michelle. "Brown Bag Lunch. She came to speak about the African Burial Ground in lower Manhattan. Did you know. . . ."

As Michelle reverently cataloged the remains that had been found, and all she'd learned from the anthropologist's talk, Neelam wondered if the length of her lover's response was a deliberate attempt to fend off more questions. Neelam didn't want to compete with information about ancestral history, so she listened attentively and let her own excavation session go by the wayside. She did not probe further. She put her faith in believing that this was a flirtation that would soon lose its newness and dissipate.

The day after the announcement of the new same-sex marriage law, over breakfast, Neelam asked, "When shall we do it? End of summer? Autumn?"

Michelle had been up for a couple of hours already—grading papers. At her feet was a stack of essays on *Their Eyes Were Watching God*. She should have handed them to her students earlier, but last-minute committee work had set her back and she was desperately trying to catch up.

Her pen skipped down the margins, inserting one-word comments:

Explain.

"Do what?"

Develop.

"Get married."

Confusing.

Michelle's pen kept moving down the page. "Oh. The fall, I think. Yes, the fall." But it was too late; Neelam had caught the beat of hesitation—the *I'm not sure* between the *Oh* and *the fall*...

The appropriate response would have been for Michelle to put down her pen, to look at her lover and say something like, "I can't believe this is a conversation we're having for real. That we're going to get married! A legal ceremony. A Justice of the Peace."

Then Neelam might have responded with something like, "I don't care when we do it, just as long as it is exactly as we want it." But this did not happen. Instead, Neelam walked across the livingroom and pretended to look out of the dirty window. She imagined Michelle perched on her desk, looking at her students who were, in turn, staring blankly at this scene, with a disembodied voice interjecting: *What is happening here?*

If their shared text was *When shall we marry?* then what was their private subtext?

Neelam went into the kitchen, leaving her lover to scribble *explain*, *develop*, *confusing* in the margins of student papers. A sparrow was trapped inside her ribcage. She put on the kettle, just to have something to occupy her mind as she waited for the small bird beneath her skin to calm down. Would a student of English Literature have known about the sparrow trapped inside her ribcage by studying a character who was waiting for a kettle to boil?

The next day, Michelle put a sign on her door and cut her office hours short. She caught the subway to the Diamond District. It was a waste of time. She could ignore the tackiness, but she couldn't ignore store after store of engagement rings that made her think about the lives of South-African miners. She got back on the subway and went further downtown. On Spring Street there was a jewelry store that sold its own designs. In the window were attractive rings—no diamonds, lots of imagination—but pricier than she was expecting.

"The rings in this tray are our simplest designs. I think of them as our classics." The assistant was barely out of high school. She had a ring in her eyebrow, another in her nose, and about half a dozen from her upper ear to her lobe. She even had a stud in her tongue, which made her look like she was sucking on a bullet.

"Can I see that tray? Those two rings there."

"These are made from Thai silver, dipped in white gold. Nice choice." Neither ring looked like a conventional wedding ring; they were both spirals made to wrap around a finger. Somewhere deep in Michelle's mind was the thought that if the marriage didn't work out, she could still wear the ring, since it didn't announce itself as a wedding band. Neelam's ring finger was the same size as hers, so if a ring wrapped around hers comfortably, then it would do for both of them.

"I'll take them."

"Both?"

"Yeah, two brides."

"Oh. Cool."

That evening, Michelle said, "Close your eyes and open your hands."

Neelam felt the small velvet box and knew what was inside it. Her first thought was, isn't this something we're supposed to pick out together? She flipped open the velvet box, acknowledged the ring's unusual beauty and said, "Let's put them away until we formally slip them on each other's fingers, okay?" She took both boxes and put them in the same place in the closet that held her sari.

Michelle shrugged. "How about dinner out tonight? It'll be my treat."

"It's always your treat."

"Come on, Nee. Let's not kill this. We can even go to that chocolatier in the East Village. Bring home truffles."

She did not want to wait until Neelam got her American qualification to practice midwifery for the next chapter of her life to begin. For a while, she hadn't minded being the one who always treated, but recently, she had been pining for someone who could surprise her with occasional tickets to Lincoln Center concerts or a Film Festival or a selection of treats at the Caribbean Day Parade. This pining had taken hold a little while after the Women's Studies Brown Bag lunch, and it was depleting the supply of love she had stored for her lover. In her mind, their conversations about marriage were markers for a day that would never come. In the same way that Neelam had tucked away a sari in the back of the closet, she had tucked away a future departure. She already regretted the purchase of the wedding rings.

Raquel languished in a Manhattan penthouse which, instead of a roof garden, had something that was a cross between an out-of-this-world greenhouse and a solarium. This was where the wedding ceremony would to take place. She sat down her fiancé and her personal assistant to make clear her desires. "I want to keep it small—120 guests, total. But I want the guests to be showered with so much love that they will leave this wedding feeling like they too have been sanctified!"

Her soon-to-be-wife, Maria, pasted a smile on her drawn, gothic-looking face and was happy to be swept along by Raquel's tsunami of money and delight. She nodded her head in agreement to all of her fiancé's wishes of silk suits, lobsters, lilies, etc. The tasks on Neelam's to-do list grew in number and in specificity, but she managed to get things done. By the final week, she was almost at the finish line. Five large tasks remained:

- Confirm life-size mermaid ice sculpture
- Check on bride & bride bouquets (white flowers)
- Check on centerpieces (jasmine, honeysuckle, candles)
- Check on waterlilies for indoor pond
- Confirm completion of indoor pond!

While Neelam ran around checking things off her to-do list, Raquel and Maria scheduled extra private Pilates and yoga sessions, and a daylong retreat at a women-only spa called Heaven, where they soaked in side-by-side tubs, which were followed by side-by-side massages, which then led to appointments for face-framing highlights for their already luminous hair.

Though New York does not use railroad tracks to divide people on the basis of skin color, it does have a culture of exclusion on the basis of class. Rich people hang out with other rich people, book the same personal trainers, eat in the same restaurants, and hire the same catering companies. Fitness and food is where you find The Great Divide. While the food portions of the wealthy were becoming smaller and smaller, the poorer inhabitants of the city were ordering everything super-sized. (When your next meal is not guaranteed, it seems wise to approach each meal like a low-cost banquet.)

As Neelam ran around on the wealthy couple's behalf, she carried two boiled eggs wrapped in tinfoil in her jacket pocket, which she ate whenever she had a few moments to rest. From the first day on the job, Raquel had told her to help herself to anything in the mammoth refrigerator, but just looking inside it overwhelmed her. Instead, she unwrapped her lunch at a favorite spot close by, in a children's playground, and sat quietly among the foreign-born nannies and their U.S. charges.

There is nothing lonelier than planning someone else's wedding when you are in a relationship that is dying. Neelam kept putting one tired foot in front the other until the indoor pond was complete; until the waterlilies were happily acclimated; and until the centerpieces, bouquets, and the ice sculpture were ready to be delivered.

At the end of the final pre-wedding workday, she flopped on her futon, pulled off her boots, and announced, "Because Raquel let me do the seating plan, I've arranged for us to sit under the ice mermaid's tail. I thought it would be a funny distraction."

"You want me to go?"

Neelam heard the sharpness inside this question, but her lover's face was hidden behind the computer screen. She massaged her own feet, wishing Michelle would let go of the mouse and offer to do this for her.

"Oh, come on. We can have a laugh picking this wedding party apart. Please? Don't let me suffer through this thing on my own."

"Will we be the only melanin-*infused* people at this event, or will there be other *shavings* of color?"

"I doubt that you will be the only descendant of the chocolate and almond people, but I'm pretty sure Hiroki and I will be the only ones representing the crème brûlée and cinnamon tribes. Oh, and Maria's sister is married into an Argentinian family, but I don't know what kind of food they are."

It was a private joke they'd begun when they first met— how anyone whose skin was not white had their complexion compared to food. She was keeping the jokey references going in the hope that it would soothe some of the harshness of her lover's questions.

Michelle didn't actually acquiesce to attending the wedding party, but the conversation trailed off to silence, which was how more and more of their recent conversations were ending, and this was taken to mean that she would go.

One-and-a-half pound lobsters, already cracked, were brought to the hundred and twenty guests to begin the feast. On the long chocolate / almond / crème brûlée / cinnamon table the conversation was minimal; there was an unspoken understanding that the less they spoke, the smaller the possibility that they might say something sarcastic or, god forbid, something which could be construed as envy.

Hiroki was finding it difficult to keep his mouth shut about the food presentation. When the main course was served without enough attention to the assembly of the Mahi Mahi and *julienned* vegetables—with an overkill of shrimp garnish—Neelam distracted him before he wept his disappointment into the mango *coulis*.

"It's not so bad, Hiroki. You want me to cut it up into small pieces and make a smiley face for you? We can make the shrimp into eyebrows!" Dealing with her string of American bosses had made her into an expert at snapping people out of their disappointments and managing the obsessions and compulsions of difficult personalities. And this reception was nothing if not the ridiculous crescendo of a wealthy person's obsessions and compulsions. The joke worked to coax Hiroki out of his impending tantrum. He pushed the shrimp to the edge of his plate, brushed the morsels of fish onto the end of his fork, smeared them with the mango *coulis*, and tried his best to savor each bite. From then on, the safe bet was to focus on the half-woman, half-fish made of ice.

The greenhouse/solarium was doing its job spectacularly well, and to the mermaid's despair she was slowly melting.

The guests closest to her tail began soaking up puddles of water with their silk napkins. After a while, soggy mountain ranges of pink silk stood where there had once been glasses of water, wine, and champagne.

Neelam jumped up to remedy The Big Melt.

"Where are you going? To turn off the sun?" Michelle was appalled—at the ridiculous wedding, at the revolting ice sculpture, at how readily her partner jumped up to take care of the situation, even though she was off the clock and no one had asked her to.

Though Neelam could not control the sun, she didn't want her table to be in sudden need of wedding-themed, life-saving devices. Before heading off to the kitchen to ask the caterers to wheel away the mermaid (whose nipples had begun to weep into the Cherry Jubilee Flambé), she whispered into Michelle's ear, "I know these tiny flames in the dessert will extinguish themselves without any help from her melting breasts, but I thought I'd be considerate and get her out of here."

Within minutes, the distorted mermaid was being wheeled away. In her absence was a damp spot of fabric that looked like a flattened globe. By this time, no one really cared what the table looked like. Damp patches under the arms of a number of guests were becoming more prominent as they danced a retro Electric Slide. In addition to the place where the mermaid had once been, there was another empty space—Michelle's chair.

THE ART OF CHANCE

There is a small yellow house with a red door. In the window boxes are yellow pansies. Around the perimeter is a row of red geraniums. The house is in the middle of a tiny village in New England. It all seems so perfect it doesn't seem real. It is not so strange that this house seems unreal; it belongs to a woman who illustrates children's books. She paints meaning in a rainbow of colors to make learning more striking.

Inside this little yellow house with an oxblood door, the woman is making a salad. She chops vegetables into a glass salad bowl, and the clear vessel allows in the light, which illuminates the red and yellow peppers.

She is learning to see vegetables according to the season and not by what is available in supermarket refrigerators. She is learning the relationship of weather to the first shoot of lettuce. She is learning how the growth of carrots is dependent on the quality of the soil. She is learning to see animals in relation to love—last night her black and white cat used her legs as a hammock; this morning she watched two Blue Jays bully the other birds, pushing the smaller ones away from the hanging feeder.

This woman in this little yellow house is now tearing apart lettuce; her hands are clean but she still has a little paint under her fingernails. In addition to illustrating children's books, she paints still lifes and portraits. Her overalls are covered in abstraction—red, yellow, and green paint adorns the denim covering her stomach and hips. Unlike her paintings, her overalls are testimony to The Art of Chance.

Another thing this woman is learning is how planting an extra row of lettuce can be a hungry person's free salad. She is grateful for this knowledge, as she is trying to pay more attention to local, smaller devastations as well as to the international and the big.

Today, for example, a total of eighty-thousand killings, spanning twenty-five years, were forced to a bloody end by the largely Buddhist government of Sri Lanka. She understands the original impulse for protest from the Hindu Tamil minority; to be starved of your language can feel like being starved of food.

This woman in this little yellow house is now chopping a red onion and humming "Morning Has Broken." She layers the onion over torn lettuce and strips of peppers, douses everything in olive oil and vinegar, then tosses the salad until all the colors shine. She does this while the rest of the villagers are outside planting lupines, lilies, and peonies. Once the villagers finish with their flower gardens, they will move to their vegetable patches. Local activists have launched a campaign—*Grow An Extra Row*—and everyone who has the money to do so is planting extra tomatoes, cucumbers, squash, etc. to help feed neighbors who might otherwise go hungry.

Early this morning she, too, planted an extra row of vegetables for New England's hungry, and as she did this she thought of the twenty-three people who were killed in three different locations in the city of Kirkuk. (Eight people were killed at a meeting of the Awakening Council; three were killed while applying for jobs in the police station; and twelve were killed in the outdoor market while shopping for red peppers and onions, and lettuce for their salads.) Though she is learning about the relationship of soil to growing, and the relationship of humans to animals, she is finding it impossible to balance local, small devastations with the international and big. This morning she is trying to balance the taking of twenty-three Iraqi lives against the annihilation of 80,000 Sri Lankans. So far, she is failing at this endeavor. In addition to planting vegetable seeds, she wants to bury her head in the soil.

Her little yellow house has its own homemade flag—a flag she has reinvented to radiate love. It is made from a bolt of yellow fabric, and on this sunny rectangle instead of a rattlesnake she has painted a baby turtle. The bubble above the turtle's head reads *Don't tread on me*, but instead of generating fear, it reminds all passersby to be tender with one another— to tiptoe.

In her twenties, she'd hid behind a low wall on the Sri Lankan coastline waiting for giant sea turtles to come ashore to lay their eggs. She watched the sea turtles release their eggs into the sand, carefully maneuvering their giant bodies to ensure their eggs remained safe and whole, to ensure that each of their babies survived. What she remembers most is how tenderly these large creatures moved to avoid stepping on their young; it was as if they were walking on tiptoe.

By inventing her own flag, the woman in the little yellow house has put Great Care on a pedestal. And why not? She is, after all, a children's book illustrator.

Last month, for a special event, she was also asked to be her village's photographer. She attended The Vintage Fashion Show fundraiser and photographed the ten successive decades (1880 to 1980) on display. As the local women and men modeled the fashions in ten-year increments, she photographed their dresses, their suits, undergarments, and hats. Before the models took to the stage to promenade and twirl in the attire of a specific decade, the narrator gave a ten-year overview of local and world history at that time. Each ten-year increment brought its own war—over this 100-year period, war was always raging somewhere in the world. For some of these decades, the attire was fashioned by death— men entered in military uniforms and women in the black clothes of mourning.

In her twenties, when she thought of roses she thought of gardens in England. Then she visited Nuwara Eliya—Sri Lanka's "Little England." (There is always a "Little" or a "New" England wherever the English land because there is no stopping them in their pursuit of larger and larger gardens.) In this city, a mile up a mountain, the temperature was cool enough for colonists to build homes with accompanying rose gardens. As Tamils and Sinhalese picked tea together on plantations, red roses bloomed on manicured colonial squares of green Sri Lankan lawns.

Her visit was before their civil war began. She stayed with a Sinhalese family who were Buddhists—a faith about which she knew nothing. So when she picked jasmine from the family's garden, their child stood paralyzed by witnessing her act of violence. After a few seconds, the little girl ran inside to her mother, "Amma, Amma, our visitor has killed a flower."

The mother of the child looked embarrassed. Their visitor looked mortified. The jasmine could not be put back. The scent of shame hung around both women's necks.

At the Vintage Fashion Show fundraiser, the woman squatted in the aisle as the models walked towards her in their costumes. While her camera focused on the details of each garment, her mind focused on war. By the time the last model emerged in an ostrich-feathered hat, she'd lost the desire to keep shooting. As she stepped out of the church and into the street, her yellow flag was waving, but in place of the baby turtle, a Tamil woman, wearing a jasmine garland, was pleading, *Don't tread on me.*

This morning, one of the twelve people killed in the Kirkuk market was a woman who had come to buy cucumbers, ci-lantro, and lettuce for the evening's salad. Beside the woman's body, the photograph showed the lettuce leaves spattered with blood. Another one of the twelve people killed in the market was a woman who had come to buy Mohammed's Flower to make rosewater. Each year, she had made this rose essence to add to her sweet rice recipes, her halva, and the dishes to commemorate her mother's passing—another woman accidentally caught by enemy gunfire.

Inside the small yellow house with an oxblood door, in a tiny New England village, the woman is still tossing her salad, thinking about how many women have been killed by accidental gunfire. She is still trying to balance the accidental loss of one life against the deliberate obliteration of the many, when her phone rings. She rushes towards the ringing with the salad bowl in her hands, and trips over her cat. She is still holding the bowl as she crashes to the floor. The fall is fast. And slow. Shards scatter and bounce. One cuts a vein in her neck. Blood pools around her body on the livingroom floor.

Outside, the yellow flag waves to all who pass by, prompting them to tiptoe, as the red geraniums lift their tender heads to the striking sun.

Pork is Love

It began as a challenge. I walked up to her at the end of the service and I said, "Poetry, poetry, blah, blah. If you want to convince me of love, then you'll stop reciting poems from the pulpit and you'll find a way to preach a sermon about pork fat." I was already standing in the doorway, shaking her hand. "If you can find a way to preach Pork Fat is Love, then I'll come back to church to hear what else you've got to say."

Her body expanded. She looked taller, wider, stronger. Oh Lord, I thought, she's gonna try to meet it. She's gonna do her damnedest to find a way to preach about pork fat and love. You know why? Because she thinks she's got her God on her side.

While she went home to study her bible or feed the hungry or do whatever else pastors do on Sunday afternoons, I thought, well, I have my own sacred ritual waiting for me at home. Pork is God to me. A useful God. One that can add flavor to practically everything and make it taste better. Even ice cream. I bought myself a cone with a scoop of Maple Bacon ice cream in Cape Cod last year. On the last vacation me and Cassie took together. Bits of bacon in my ice cream made me happy. If the world were cooked in pork fat, I think it would be a happier place. But the Muslims don't eat it and there are a whole lot of them. And the Jews don't eat it and there are plenty of them. And the Hindus are all vegetarians and there are masses of them. And the Atheists and the Agnostics are multiplying these days and they both have more than their fair share of vegetarians, so pork goes out the window there. And then there are the environmentalists who want to Save the Planet with Meatless Mondays. So, right there, I can add a whole bunch of people to my personal list of the Godless.

Thank God for meat-eating Christians.

Thank *both* Gods—the one in heaven, the one at the trough.

I don't let anyone into my cabin. I don't want them to see my altar—eighty mason jars full of pork fat. People think that pork fat is pork fat, but if it were, then all of my jars would be full of the exact same color of the white stuff. I can testify, that's not true. Pork fat has different colors—my jars have striations.

In my kitchen I have a long wooden shelf at eye-level. This shelf continues along three of the kitchen walls. On it, perfectly lined up, sits one Mason jar after another, each one full to the brim. (Except for the last one—number eighty—that one is still collecting my latest dribs and drabs.) When the sun streams through my kitchen window, it lights up my jars and highlights the striations. This is my stained-glass window.

On the day Cassie left, the house was still full of her. Then summer turned into fall, and like leaves on late November trees she dropped out of my life. The wind swept away what was left of her. Gone was her smell on the pillows. Gone were the leftovers in the freezer. Gone was her stock of canned goods for the winter. I was down to a handful of potatoes and a pound of bacon. Then I was down to no potatoes and half a pound of bacon. And that's when it began.

I ate nothing for the whole day. Then just before bedtime I cooked up the last of the bacon, ate it in bed, pushed the empty plate away, and put my head on the pillow that had once smelled of her. When I woke up the next day the bedroom smelled of bacon and it comforted me. On my lunch hour, I stopped in at the smokehouse and I bought enough bacon to last me a week. I pledged an oath: from this day forward I will eat nothing all day, then I will eat as much bacon as I can stomach just before bed. And I did. My pillow smelled of God. Pork fat lulled me to sleep, nudged me awake, and most of all, it lifted me up.

Just before Christmas, I opened my mailbox to find: *The Most Important Gift Catalog In The World.* It was from Feed A Family International. Inside it said:

GIVE THE GIFT OF A PIG: $120

If you are looking for a present that will leave your friends, family, or co-workers squealing with delight this holiday season, look no further than the gift of a pig.

I looked over my shoulder on the way back to my cabin from the mailbox. Was someone watching me through my kitchen window? I'd been feeling that a lot lately, like someone knows what I'm up to, what I'm thinking. It started after the last service, when Pastor Adebayo had finished reciting that poem. I think it was called, *A Disaster.* It was about losing stuff—keys, watches, etc. But then it got a bit strange. It's hard to keep up with a poem when you're hearing it for the first time and you only get to hear it once. Also, Pastor Adebayo has a thick accent—a mix of British English with some kind of African accent thrown in—so every time she said the line that kept repeating "the art of losing isn't hard to master" her accent threw me off . . . *disAHster, mAHster* . . . I started thinking about stuff I'd lost, instead of paying attention to the words. I'm pretty sure someone in the poem lost a house or two. No details, like if the houses got swept up in a hurricane or if they burned down to the ground.

Houses burn down a lot around here; it happens when they're made of wood. And the electric is old. Or if it's night and people have let the woodstove go out and put on the propane heater instead. Houses that burn down by accident are one of the reasons I've kept visitors at bay. I'm used to my propane heater. But if a guest comes over, I could have myself a disastrous chain of events: a wayward movement, a fire, the whole cabin up in flames.

That's kind of how I felt when I came home to find Cassie had gone—like there'd been some wayward movement that accidentally set a fire. Her leaving was like an accident. Like she didn't really want to go, more like I'd somehow accidentally pushed her out.

She left a note. A short one. (She knows that words aren't my thing.)

Jay,

I don't wish you any harm. I'm not even that angry. I do get a little angry when I think of how long it's taken me to leave. But I'm trying to forgive myself. And I hope, if you need to, you will forgive yourself too. I still feel love for you, I just can't keep living this tucked-away-life. I need something different, something more.

Please don't look for me, Jay. I want to figure out what I want on my own. Please let me go.

With love (still),
Cassie

Accidentally or not, losing her burned me right down to the ground. And when I was nothing but ashes, a hurricane came along and scattered what was left of me all over the county. I was a complete disaster. Which surprised me. Because even though we were together for twenty years, at least one day each week I woke up wondering: *Is today gonna be the day she leaves me? The day that she thinks: I can't take one more minute.*

What comes as a shock and what I expect to happen are alive inside me at the same time—running parallel. I've always known this. But still, Cassie's leaving blindsided me, made me unsteady and even more reluctant than ever to leave my cabin. I went when I was called out for odd jobs, but I only accepted as many as I needed to keep all my bills paid. It was easy to avoid conversations with the people I worked for—they really just wanted me to fix whatever needed fixing as quickly as I could. More often than not they made me coffee. Asked if I wanted cream, sugar. Sometimes they offered me a snack. I did a good job and got out of their houses and back to my home as fast as I could. After a few months of this, my nights alone got longer. And I was sleeping less and less. On the sleepless nights, it even felt hard to breathe.

Eventually, a week or so after the sermon, I made my way to Pastor Adebayo's to talk. It wasn't easy. I'm not much of a talker. I also had to get over the fact that she was the only person I had to turn to. I'd done such a good job of keeping to myself that I had no friends. I felt like if I didn't tell someone that Cassie had left me, I might die of exhaustion from lack of sleep or from struggling to breathe.

I liked that the pastor didn't look surprised when I showed up at the parsonage. How she welcomed me into her home without asking any questions. And I liked how she had the woodstove burning. I wondered what it must be like to live in a place where a woodstove is needed—after growing up in Nigeria. I didn't even know if they had snow in Nigeria.

"Who splits your wood?" I asked.

"I do."

"I bet you didn't learn that in Africa, did you?

"I've learned a lot of things here that I didn't learn in Nigeria. How about you?

"I learned to split wood from my father."

"I meant, are there things you've learned from a place where you didn't grow up?"

"Nope. I've been in Vermont for my whole life. I watch a lot of TV, though, so I've learned a few things that way."

She relaxed into her wing-back chair like she had no other plans. "TV counts. What have you learned from it?"

Instead of talking to a pastor, I felt like I was meeting with a professor. She had something collegey about her. I felt put on the spot. She was surrounded by the things she'd learned—the split wood, the woodstove, books on every religion under the sun—while I had to wrack my brain to come up with something. I shifted to the edge of my chair, thinking about how I could make an excuse to leave.

"Would you like some tea?" She didn't wait for me to respond before pouring the tea she'd already brewed.

"I've learned that the Queen of England has lots of Corgis."

"Corgis? So you love dogs?"

"Yes I do. For all the right reasons."

"And what are the right reasons?"

"They love you. And they're obedient."

"Ah, obedience. Is that important to you?"

I heard myself slurp the tea. She had her back to me as she crouched to feed wood into the stove, but I felt like she had eyes in the back of her head.

"I said obedience *and* love. Both of these things—together. I'm like most people, I guess. I like knowing what to expect—coming home from work at the same time, dinner at the same time. I'm not much for surprises."

"Is that what brings you here? You're troubled by a surprise?"

The word was likely out. You can't keep things hidden for long and it had been months since Cassie had left. Someone must have noticed she'd stopped going by the general store to pick up the bread on Mondays, or the eggs and milk on Tuesdays. Or that she'd stopped going by the smokehouse on Wednesdays. Someone must have noticed and mentioned it to Pastor Adebayo—otherwise how else would she have brought up the subject of troubling surprises minutes into my visit?

"Well, Cassandra's gone. She left a note, but I still don't know why. She said she wants me to let her go. I'm not sure how I can let her go when she's the one who left me. I don't even know where she is. But her note says, *Please let me go.*

And that please confuses me. It's as if I had a say in her leaving. But I didn't. I've lost her, Pastor. And I don't mean lost like when someone you love dies. And I don't mean lost like when you can't find your keys. Or like when you lose yourself in a chore and half the day has gone. It's bigger than that. It's like that disaster poem you read in church. It's like I've lost a river or a country. Sounds stupid, I know."

Somewhere in the middle of me spilling my guts, Pastor Adebayo had shut her eyes. I've got to get out of here, I thought. This was a mistake. I stood up.

"Where are you going?"

"I shouldn't have come. I'm not good at talking."

"But I haven't responded yet. Give us a chance at this."

"You don't know me. I don't know you. I don't know what I'm doing here. Besides, I'm putting you to sleep."

"I close my eyes to listen, not to be distracted. I wasn't just listening to what you had to say. I was also listening to how you sound. There's nothing stupid about the loss of a loved one feeling like you've lost a river. And there's certainly nothing stupid about their absence feeling like the loss of a country. It's been a few years since I've been home, but the last time I was, the African continent had lost an entire country with a population double the size of Vermont's. And I don't mean lost as in absent or mislaid. I mean lost as in dead. Gone. Even so, a loved one leaving you is also a big thing. It has its own kind of grief. Don't you think I understand?"

This little speech of hers gave me pause. I sat back down. We were eye to eye.

"So how do I sound?"

"Wounded."

"Like a dog?"

"No, Jay, like a person."

The sound of *Jay* coming of her mouth surprised me. I hadn't heard someone speak my name for so long.

"Love is not guaranteed. Still, we choose it. And when we do, we do so knowing we run the daily risk of losing it. Yes?"

What was I supposed to say to that? Her collegey voice was confusing me. I felt comfortable and uncomfortable at the same time—running parallel. I had come to her for some sympathy, some building up. I wanted help to gather myself back together. I didn't want her asking me questions that were breaking the pieces of me into smaller bits.

I pulled my hat down over my ears. "I've got to go." She looked surprised, but she didn't look concerned. She didn't ask me to stay. She walked me to the door like a good host, patting my shoulder as if she were saying, *Do what you need to do.*

By the time I got back to my cabin it was already dark, close to the time to fry up my dinner, but the visit to Pastor Adebayo's had taken away my appetite. I didn't even try to cook the bacon. I just got under the covers, stared at the ceiling, and let my stomach growl.

Me and Cassie hadn't had a dog in years. I don't know why I brought up the Queen's Corgis. And what did I really feel about obedience and love? I don't think I'd given either of them any thought. In the twenty years that Cassie and me were together, more and more things would come flying out of my mouth as if I'd meant to say them, but they surprised me as much as they surprised (or shocked) whoever I was talking to. When we were in public, Cassie would save me from myself, explain away whatever odd thing had jumped out before I could catch it. But when it was just the two of us, instead of saving me, she'd force me to explain myself.

The day before I found her note, she had done just that: "What did you just say?"

"I said pork fat is love."

"And how did you come to that conclusion?"

"Is there anything else we save in a jar after it's been used? It sits on that shelf looking like something we worship."

She held up my latest jar. It was fresh grease, still liquid. She tilted it, watching the contents move from side to side. "Twenty years and I still don't know where you get half your ideas. Most days, you barely venture further than the front yard. Sometimes I think you don't need the rest of the world. Just you and your imagination and you're happy."

She had a point. A lot of what I say sounds as if it is random. But it isn't. It's just that the journey from my heart to my head to my mouth is a long zigzag and anyone listening might think I've lost my way. Cassie was nothing like me. She always knew how to handle words, putting serious ones inside a funny sentence to make sure I would listen. The last thing she said to me was the same day that she tilted the jar of liquid pork fat. "If I felt like messing with you, I could put this jar by your tea with a spoon in it and you'd think it was honey. So you'd better be careful when you accuse me." Even though she was kidding, it was true. She could have easily tricked me into thinking the grease was honey. Cassie had lived with me long enough to know that half the time I was pretending to listen, while my mind was thinking about stacking wood before the first snow or planting the vegetable garden after the last frost.

But since she left me, I couldn't care less if the wood stayed unstacked all winter, and as for vegetables, well, now I don't have much use for them. Give me bacon and I'm good to go.

I didn't listen to her enough. Too much in my own head. She must have been lonely in this cabin, on top of this hill, away from the village. *I* did this to her. It was *me* who pushed everyone away.

I'm sure the villagers must be wondering what took her so long to leave me. When I'm lying sleepless in my bed I imagine all the people in town, huddled around fireplaces, talking about me. It's not that I think that the people down there don't have better things to do—they do—but gossip is the Devil's Radio and it broadcasts to those who have the time to listen. And there are an awful lot of people here—living on inherited wealth or comfortable retirements—who have little else to fill their days.

I wonder how many of them got the catalogue from Feed A Family International? If any of them bought a pig as a present for a family in Romania? I wish I had more money. If I had more I'd buy a "Pig As A Present" for every family in an entire Romanian village. I still might buy one pig, for one family at least, but I worry that the family in Romania may never get it. Do Romanians even eat pork? It feels like no one does these days. My granddad used to kill a pig every November and it would feed us all through a long Green Mountain winter. According to the Feed A Family catalogue, they still do this in the places I've never visited. It makes me want to go to these countries to hand-deliver pigs to those who most need them. Maybe if I did, I'd find Cassie living with a Romanian family, using every scrap of pork fat, chatting away to people who don't lose their thoughts on the long, zigzaggy roads from their hearts to their heads to their mouths. And who don't pretend to listen. I bet she knew this catalogue would arrive and that I'd read it. Maybe that's why her note said, *Please don't look for me, Jay . . . Please let me go.*

A couple of days after my abrupt leaving, I went back to Pastor Adebayo's. Her dog was outside, barking, guarding her chickens. Her lights were on. As I walked up the drive she came out to greet me. We walked back into her house in silence, like we were both waiting to be inside to pick up the conversation where we'd left off.

Before I sat down, I pulled out the Feed A Family catalogue and handed it to her to look at. "Is this for real? If I buy a pig will the family really get it? Do they eat pork in Romania?"

She laughed so much I thought she was going to bust a blood vessel. I laughed with her because it's difficult not to when someone else is laughing hard. While I was laughing, I was thinking: Wait a minute, am I laughing at myself? And if I am, what's so damn funny?

Then she said, "Yes, I think people eat pork in Romania. There are lots of scams out there, but this catalogue isn't one of them. Are you seriously going to give the gift of a pig? Is that why you want me to preach about pork and love? I'm humbled. Truly I am. I thought you were just, oh, I don't know, testing me. Sorry for laughing. The catalogue took me by surprise. When it came into *my* letterbox last week, I couldn't get beyond the advertising copy. A present that will leave your friends and family *squealing* with delight? I know someone must've thought *squealing* was a clever word choice, but all I could see was the poor animal being slaughtered. Yes, the catalogue is for real. What a generous and thoughtful gift!"

As she walked me to the door, she announced, "This Sunday, no poems. Promise. I will do my best to honor your request. I will preach a sermon about pork fat and love. Please. Come."

When Sunday came around, I wasn't ready. I'd run out of toothpaste, and I had a pimple on my chin—probably from the masses of fat I'd been eating. I was a complete disaster. I brushed my teeth with a paste of water and baking soda, put on a clean shirt, and walked down the winter hill. Snow had coated everything. The spire was visible because it was set against the sunny sky, but the rest of the church blended into the landscape, as if there were no boundaries between its walls and the outdoors. I was almost the last parishioner to arrive.

Pastor Adebayo was popular. She regularly filled the church to a capacity that none of the previous pastors had managed. You had to admire someone who had come from the outside, from another country even, and got local people to trust her with their faith. She was welcoming and had a low tolerance for baloney. If gossip was the Devil's Radio, then she tried her best to keep the power supply hidden, especially from the town clerk who looked like an angel, but behaved like an evil Town Crier. Once, while the clerk was broadcasting the latest news about the general store owners' teenage boys—who were breaking into village houses and stealing power tools to sell on eBay—the pastor pulled the plug by putting her finger up to the clerk's lips to shush the woman. She had some drama to her, the pastor, and I enjoyed watching her show.

When the pastor stood in the pulpit the church fell silent. "Good morning. I hope you are all feeling well and ready to embrace this new day. Prepare yourselves for something a little different this morning."

As she walked towards the dais there was a tiny bit of fidgeting from the congregation. In the center of the raised area she'd already placed a hostess cart, and she positioned herself behind it. From the second shelf of the cart she pulled out a small camping stove and a frying pan. She placed the burner on top of the cart and set the pan on top of that. She lit the burner and suddenly all eyes were on the flame.

"This morning I want you to think of God's love as this blue flame. And this frying pan as the world we inhabit."

The congregation sat transfixed, waiting for her next move. She pulled out a piece of meat—a slab of pork! I snickered. The town clerk looked round to register who had made the sound. I wanted to stick my tongue out at her like some overgrown kid, but instead I gave her the evil eye, and she whipped her head back around to the front.

"Imagine yourself as this piece of pork," said the pastor.

Some people laughed. Some people froze. I thought I was going to burst. She held up the raw meat like a magician and made sure everyone got a good view of it before she tossed it into the pan. The pork sizzled. In this moment, sizzling meat in this church sounded like the loudest sound in the world. She moved the pork around the pan with a fork and spoke above the sound. "When you are born you are tossed into your life, a life that is sustained by the blue flame of God. If you do not watch over this flame, it will be extinguished. If you turn it up high, the meat will burn. If you turn it down too low, it will take too long to cook and you run the risk of being left with something that is tasteless and dry. But if you tend to your life, keep turning yourself over, and adjusting the temperature, the flame of God will transform you, as this piece of meat is now transformed. The flame of God helps you to become something more than you once were. Like this." She held the cooked slab of pork in midair, its juices dripping.

She had captivated the congregation with her sermon and the smell of pork. I heard a growling stomach in the pew in front of me. I wanted to stand up and testify, *Hallelujah for Pork!* But I didn't want to draw attention to myself.

She put the pork onto a plate and began to slice it.

"As I cut up this meat, the plate fills with juice—full of goodness, something to save. How many of us save these juices in a jar by our stove to add to future recipes? After these juices cool and transform into something solid—fat—we go back to them, scoop out a helping to add to our future dishes to give them more flavor, yes?"

I looked around. People were nodding in agreement. I wasn't alone.

"A short while ago, I read a poem to you about how easy it is to lose something we love—from something as small as a mother's watch to something as large as a continent. Today's sermon is about how we can keep something we value safe— something small, like pork fat in a jar, or something large, like love in our hearts. We all know how easy it can be to lose something we hold dear, yes? So, for this week, let us practice keeping something we love safe. When you look at that jar—a solid store of something that you can dip into, something that a simple flame can melt—let pork fat remind you of love."

She'd done it, preached the sermon. No poetry, just pork.

I waited behind to thank her, but some small emergency required her to go into the back of the church. I didn't hang around. I wrapped myself up in my cold-weather layers and headed back up the hill. The snow was falling steadily, swirling about my face. Sometimes the world feels tight and small, as though God has trapped me inside a snow globe. But on my walk home, the casing had lifted, and my walk through the snow was a release.

As I stepped over my threshold, out of the cold and into the heat, there was no denying it, my cabin felt raw. No amount of frying bacon was going to bring Cassie back. She wasn't hiding out in Romania. I might not have known her as well as I thought, but I didn't think she would have made that much of a change. She had begun a new life somewhere other than here, that was for sure. I had to accept it and get back to a regular way of eating—three meals, with bread, with potatoes and other veggies.

By the next evening, the snow had reached my window boxes. It was one of those nights when no one in their right mind would venture out. In the valley, the lights from my neighbors' windows glowed. I had some baby-back ribs in barbecue sauce in the oven. Almost done. I forced myself to cook up some greens.

As I threw the greens into the pot, there was a knock. At first I thought my ears were playing tricks, but when it happened again, accompanied by the sound of a muffled hello, I hurried to answer it. There, at my door, was Pastor Adebayo with a tote bag in her hand.

"Pastor? What are you doing out in this weather!"

"I came with a gift. Please, call me Dora."

"Couldn't it have waited?"

"No, actually, it couldn't. It's food. I just made it. It's probably not hot-hot, but it will still be warm."

She put the bag down on the chair and took off her gloves and hat, and unwound her scarf. She hung her things near the woodstove to dry. The heat melted the snow on her hat and scarf, and the drips made small pools on the floor.

She took the dish out of the bag and handed it to me.

"Thank you! What is it?"

"*Awala.* It is a dish from home, made from yam flour. I make it when I am feeling homesick. It goes well with—well, practically everything."

"Good, because you're just in time for dinner. Sit."

"I brought it because I wanted to say thank you for inspiring me, and because I wanted to give you something you've never tasted before, from somewhere you've never been."

Dora sat. She kept my house full of words, chatting, offering me little morsels of information about her homeland, like how it only had two seasons—the rainy and the dry. The collegey part of her voice had evaporated; instead she sounded like someone who wanted someone else to talk to. I closed my eyes for a second so that I could concentrate on how she sounded: lonely.

I finished setting the table, dished out the ribs, the greens, the *awala.*

I lit a candle.

As we ate, the flame burned slightly blue.

OSMAN'S WINDOW

Once he got to Maine, the Refugee Relocation Center helped him find a place to live, a room in an apartment with three other Somali men. Two of them shared a bedroom. Osman and the fourth man had bedrooms of their own. In his entire twenty-two years on this earth, he had never had his own room. Back home, he had shared one room with his three brothers, and in the refugee camps he had shared a succession of tents with many, many other Bantu—not just men, but women also—to protect each other from late-night attacks. In his new room, there was one bed with a small table beside it, and pressed up against the shortest wall there was a chest with six drawers for his clothing, though what he owned couldn't even fill two.

When he closed his bedroom door to sleep, it shut out all sound except for his own breath. The solitude unnerved him. He lulled himself to sleep by placing his ear to the wall that linked him to the second bedroom, listening to the sleeping breath and the occasional snore of his roommates.

The apartment was above a halal grocery store on the main street. On the other side of the street were a number of stores that were run by more of his countrypeople. From the window of his apartment, he could see the Mogadishu Business Center, which offered various services: tailoring, cleaning, and money transfers. For the first few days, he pulled a chair close to the livingroom window and watched his Bantu brothers and sisters walking beside white people along the main thoroughfare, buying fish, oats, vegetables, and even clothes, and it looked to him as if he had landed in a place of miracles.

He'd arrived a little too early for snow. Even so, from the window he saw Bantus going about their new Maine days bundled up in coats and boots and hats. Though his apartment included heat, he wrapped a scarf around his neck and pulled a woolen hat down over his ears just so that he could feel like he was one of the crowd. The newness of America, especially the cold, gave him hope that he could push away the bad memories that came with hot days.

By the third day of sitting in an empty apartment, watching people walk by, his roommates declared the window Osman's Window. One of them hung a blanket over the chair and even moved a small table beneath it for Osman to rest his tea. Osman wouldn't have dreamed of sectioning off any part of their apartment and calling it his, but his roommates never sat in that chair or covered themselves with the blanket. Their tenderness towards him made him want to cry.

These men were not only careful with him, they were careful with each other. Tentative gestures that came from a lifetime of uncertainty filled the apartment: they walked barefoot over carpeted floors, often surprising one another coming out of a bedroom, their bodies wincing in response; they stirred the sugar in their tea as quietly as they could, as if the sound of spoons clinking against mugs could wake a sleeping predator.

In just one week the Refugee Relocation Center found Osman a job in a small facility that produced handcrafted chocolates. The couple that had begun the enterprise (part factory, part storefront) was also from another country. "Twenty years!" said Tulio Medina. "But with every bit of chocolate we import, we have found a way to bring a little bit of Venezuela to Maine. And this makes us very happy! We hope that you too, Osman, will find some happiness here. Welcome!"

Tulio and Rita Medina both had mothers who had taught them how to make a variety of chocolate-based desserts, and years later, here they were, with their own employees, creating heir own variations, and selling their Bean-to-Bar and shaped confectioneries to gourmet stores all over the U.S., to Mainers, and to tourists who wandered in to buy their loved ones a special treat.

Rita took her time introducing Osman to all the ingredients. She asked him to taste the cream, the fruit, the herbs, and the flowers. She offered him a chocolate that looked like a small sea creature. When he bit into it, a pink cream covered his tongue that tasted like the red berry he had just sampled.

"What you have there, Osman, is a raspberry cream seahorse, molded out of dark chocolate, with a dusting of sea salt. Everything that you have just seen has been artfully made into this perfect taste. Your job will be to pack the chocolate boxes. You understand?"

Osman could not respond to Rita because his mouth was still full of something so perfect that he was afraid to open it in case the taste escaped and never returned.

"Good," she continued, ushering him through an aisle of trays of perfectly molded chocolates, stacked on metal racks, from floor to ceiling. The chocolates were a variety of shapes and sizes, some of which looked like they'd been decorated with gold.

When they got to what Rita called The Floor, there were a couple of long tables with people standing behind them, filling chocolate boxes. The six women and three men, all of them white-skinned, smiled at Osman. The whiteness of their faces, the whiteness of the walls, the whiteness of the tables and the uniforms, blended into one large cloud that restricted his breath. He put one hand over the other and then over his heart to try to calm its pounding. Why had the Refugee Relocation Center not found him a job with his own people—in the halal grocery store or at the Mogadishu Restaurant or anywhere where he would have had at least one Bantu man or woman to talk to? He wanted to run, but he could not be ungrateful to all of the white people who had done so much for him—given him a home, found him work. And so he smiled back at his new co-workers. As he did this, all nine employees put their hands over their own hearts, thinking it was his way of greeting them.

Their eagerness to welcome him calmed him a little. He nodded his head and said hello. They nodded their heads and helloed him back.

At the far end of The Floor was a wooden lectern with wings carved out from its edges. The winged lectern held an open newspaper. Rita ushered him closer. "We have borrowed this idea from the Cubans, Osman. Every day begins with one hour of someone reading articles from the newspaper, while everyone else works. We take it in turns. But you don't have to read if you don't want to, or if you don't yet feel ready. Mr. Medina and I know how difficult it is to learn a new language. But if you listen to others read, it might help you to learn English more quickly, yes? For now, though, you don't have to think about anything other than putting chocolates into small boxes, okay?"

In Somalia, there had been no need for Osman to read the news in any language. The news came from the radio. Once in a while, if a wealthy neighbor felt generous enough to bring their television outside, Osman and others would squat in their front yard to watch what was going on in the world.

The wooden lectern looked like a soldier, standing guard; it made him feel uneasy.

Rita continued, "Every afternoon, for another hour, the same person will also read something else—sometimes a story, other times poems. Once, we read a mystery that went on for a number of days. Whatever the rest of the workers are in the mood for. We take a vote." Rita caught an expression of fear flit over Osman's face. "Don't worry," she said. "All you have to do is listen. It is entertainment—to make time pass more pleasurably."

Rita handed him a tiny clear plastic box. Inside were two chocolates—two dark squares decorated with golden leaves. "Take these home with you. We will see you tomorrow, bright and early?"

Once Osman got home, he placed the two chocolates on the small table under the window. He covered himself with the blanket and waited for his roommates to return, occasionally shifting his gaze from the people walking along the main street to the two little gold-topped treats.

The other three men didn't return home until night. Osman had already fallen asleep in his chair. They left him to sleep until they had finished washing off the workday from their bodies. Once they had changed into clean clothes and the room was warm from the steam of the shower and the heat of the stove, one man tapped him on the shoulder. "We have made tea."

Osman stood up slowly and yawned, stretching his arms above his head. He remembered the chocolates and fetched them from the table. "These are what my new bosses gave me." He sliced each chocolate in half, making sure that each man got to put a gold leaf into his mouth. "My job is to pack things made out of chocolate and gold."

As each man ate his tiny chocolate morsel, a relaxed conversation continued in the shared language of home.

"So working in the halal market is too good for you!" one roommate teased.

"It was not my choice, brother. This is what they have given me."

Another roommate, captivated by this new taste, nodded his head to allow the sweetness to slowly melt in his mouth.

At 9 A.M. the next day the packers at Chimbley's Chocolates stood around the white tables in the white room carefully placing dark squares decorated with gold leaves, or orange tulips, or pink flamingos, or pale pink blossoms, dusted with cocoa powder or sea salt, into clear plastic boxes held together with elasticated gold thread. Osman joined them in his new white apron and uniform-hat covering his shaved head. The employee who had been elected to read stood at the front of the room, behind the winged lectern. Her hair was neatly tucked inside her own uniform-hat. A large beauty mark above her top lip accentuated the movement of her mouth as she read the news aloud:

A black therapist in Florida trying to calm a man with autism in the middle of the street says he was shot by police, even though he had his hands in the air and repeatedly told the officers that both were unarmed.

Osman tried to catch his co-workers' reactions to this news. He could not see all their faces, but their hands placed chocolates into plastic boxes without trembling. There was a specific order to filling each box—pink blossom next to orange tulip next to pink flamingo, etc., but listening to these newspaper words—a man being shot even though his hands were raised in surrender—made his heart race, which made his hands shake, which made his feet want to run.

The woman continued to read:

The moments before the shooting were recorded on a cellphone video, showing the man lying on the ground with his arms raised, talking to his patient and police throughout the standoff with officers, who appeared to have them surrounded. "As long as I've got my hands up, they're not going to shoot me. This is what I'm thinking. They're not going to shoot me," the man told the local TV news station later from his hospital bed, where he was recovering from a gunshot wound to his leg. "Wow, was I wrong."

Osman's mind froze. Then his hands did the same. Or was it the other way around? He did not know. The news story had scrambled his insides. How could listening to these words make time pass more pleasurably? The mark above the reader's lip bounced up and down as she read. Osman tried to put his hands back to work, but he touched a chocolate too hard and a gold leaf broke away from its dark base. The co-worker to his left noticed, but did not say anything.

The worker behind the lectern kept reading: Her mouth seemed bigger, and the mark on her lip had transformed into a fly that was ready to launch itself into the air.

The shooting comes at a time of growing tensions and in-creased protests against the disproportionate number of African Americans killed by the police.

By this time, the white employees around the table had become more tentative in their packing; listening to this news with a dark-skinned man—a refugee!—in their midst had made their hands clumsier and the chocolates more fragile. This was not the first time that they had listened to articles about police officers treating black U.S. citizens unjustly, but listening to this news with Osman standing beside them made the words more difficult to stomach.

The employee behind the lectern had not yet noticed the change in the room. She was enjoying the sound of her own voice, taking pleasure in getting the pacing just right and making her enunciation smooth. She thought about what kind of training would be required to be an audio-book reader, and if that line of work paid more than packing chocolates. As she mused on this, she continued to read:

The black therapist said he was trying to calm his 23-year-old patient who had run away from the group home where he works. "All he has is a toy truck in his hand," the therapist can be heard saying in the video, speaking of his patient, who was holding a toy. "That's all it is. There is no need for guns."

Osman tried to put his hands back to work, hoping he had the chocolates in the right order, but he struggled to pay attention. His chest felt tight, his mind a blur of things he wanted to forget. He wished the lectern's wings would carry the woman and her smooth voice far away from his ears.

Eventually, the reader took a bathroom break. Another female employee followed her. When they returned, the reader closed the newspaper and took her place around the packing table. The room filled with a silence as loud as a police siren.

Osman had witnessed enough bad things to last him many lifetimes. He had lived a long while in a tent in Kakuma so that he could one day make it to America to forget about the violence: the attacks at family celebrations when everyone was awake and dancing; the attacks in the middle of the night when everyone was asleep and dreaming. Night or day, Somalia or Kenya, he had lived with the expectation that his body, or the body of someone close to him, might be destroyed. With his brothers gone (he didn't know where, and he didn't want to think about the possibility that all three were dead), and with his mother too ill to move to America with him, he wanted his Maine future to be different. He had come to begin his New Day.

Back home, boys and young men spent their free time talking about what they might do if they got a hold of a gun. They talked about guns with reverence. But for Osman, guns brought his words to a stop. When his brothers and cousins gathered to talk about their fantasies of fighting with armies, the talk of fighting made him want to dig a hole in the ground and hide. The need to protect each other from an army or rebel group was necessary. That was a fact. But when these conversations began, he slipped away unnoticed.

His own fantasies took place beside his herd of goats, making up songs. His father had taught him a couple: one about a boy who saved his own life by squatting in a field of tall grass to hide from predators; another about the full moon lighting the way to a school where children learned to put words on paper. In the latter, the written word was a gift from Allah. But for Osman, words that were sung were the real gift.

He tried to explain: "When I sing, Papa . . ."

"Come. Hold this." His father was trying to stop an injured hoof from bleeding, and he needed his son to help him keep the goat still. Father and son flanked the animal and held it until it surrendered.

Osman tried again. "Papa. . . ."

"What?"

"When I sing it is like the sun is shining inside me."

His father stopped what he was doing to look at his son. He never knew what was going to come out of Osman's mouth. Though this son was a curiosity, the father was glad that at least one of his children had inherited his singing voice. Truth be told, it surprised him that this son had not hardened, like the other three, from all that he had witnessed—fathers killed, mothers grieving. Sisters defiled. Brothers snatched.

On the nights when neighbors joined father and son on a reed-flute or a drum, the songs made Osman's body fill with a golden light, and the strength of the beat made him covet his own drum as much as his brothers coveted guns.

After his father's murder, Osman wanted to sell some of his herd to buy a musical instrument or two, but every goat was vital to his family's survival. Instead, he fashioned two ankle-rattles that made music as he walked. His pride in his homemade instruments wore off quickly, however, after one of his brothers made fun of him. "Look! Osman is sneaking away to play music with his goats!" They laughed at him. Called him a girl. They lay on their backs with their legs in the air, shaking their imaginary ankle-rattles in mockery.

"It is you who look like fools—on your backs, shaking your legs like demented animals!" And off he went, unable to stomp away in anger because the rattling would have only invited more teasing.

In the refugee camp, Osman had looked for ways to avoid sleeping. In dreams, his father transformed from a dancing wedding-guest to a murdered man in a matter of seconds.

No one had seen the soldiers enter the village. They hid among the wedding guests. Killed six of them in one short burst of gunfire. Fled into the midnight bushes. On bad nights, these few brutal moments filled an entire night's worth of sleep.

At the end of his first workday, Osman went to Tulio's office. "Mr. Medina. I want to say. . . . Thank you. Thank you. Very much. For this work. But. I cannot return."

Tulio was startled. "Has someone been bad to you? We will not tolerate intolerance at Chimbley's Chocolate. Tell me, Osman. We can fix this."

Osman was not sure what to do—should he speak the truth? Would it be an insult? Would his English be good enough? It was difficult to speak about his feelings in Maay-Maay, so how could he speak about what he felt in a language that was so new to him, and with so many words that he did not know? He wanted to tell the truth. He tried, "I cannot. Listen. To stories. With guns. For me. This is not. Pleasure." He was going to say more. But it was not necessary.

Tulio had left Venezuela after the oil crisis had turned it into a country at war with itself. He was embarrassed that Venezuela, today, was synonymous with a shortage of daily essentials, a citizenry queuing for toilet paper. He was ashamed that the place of his peaceful childhood was now known as "the most murderous place on Earth." He'd seen the violence firsthand, and it haunted him for his first few years in the U.S. Once in a while, something he wanted to forget would still wake him at night. He would pace the factory floor, counting trays of chocolate, as a way to distract his thoughts. He was not a refugee—not legally, anyway—but in his heart he felt like someone who had been forced to flee his birthplace, and his heart knew better than a court of law. "Please, Osman. Stay. We can fix this. From now on, I promise. No more stories with guns."

A month passed, and it was officially winter. Although he was a Muslim, Osman loved the way Christians in America celebrated the birth of their Savior. It was all about light—lights outside homes, lights inside homes. Trees covered with white lights. Trees covered with rainbow lights. And best of all, trees inside homes! As he walked home from Chimbley's

Chocolates, he was treated to one lighted inside-tree after another: in store windows, house windows, apartment windows.

At some point he had mentioned wanting a lighted inside-tree to his co-workers, and the woman with the mark above her lip began a secret collection to buy him a small fir and a package of white lights.

After her initial obliviousness, she had become attentive to Osman's words and gestures. Though she no longer read the articles at work that talked about the injustices against darker-skinned U.S. citizens, she was reading them to herself. With an urgency that was new to her. It was as if she had discovered a secret, except it wasn't a secret; it had been there for years—the words and images staring her in the face, from the newspaper, from the TV screen.

She started going to a small coffee shop to read the papers for free. When she saw things she knew nothing about, she went to the local library to get on the computer to Google more information. On one or two occasions, she even took a book out of the library. When she read, she read quickly, as if she were racing against time. Or trying to make up for lost time. She learned about Somali Bantus—where they'd come from, how they were mostly river people. She learned about their civil war—about the killings, the torture, the ethnic cleansing. But of all the things she learned, the thing that entered her dreams at night was the long walk to reach the Kenyan border; how on this journey so many of Bantus were eaten by lions, hyenas, and other predators. She read about how they had walked and walked, sustained only by a diet of leaves and contaminated water. She read about how their prayers were for the skies to open and bless them with rain.

Now that some of these Bantu refugees had become her neighbors, they were real to her, not just words in newspaper articles, or in books, or images on a screen. It was *this* that made the difference. Her new neighbors had survived, made it to the U.S.—a place where, at last, they hoped to find safety. But here they were, once again under threat. She realized that her co-worker could be the next dark-skinned citizen to be unjustly shot. It was the thing that changed her. The thing that woke her up.

As she bounced from newspaper article to library book to Google to Wikipedia page, she thought about what else she could do to welcome Osman. She stumbled on the need for prayer during the day and how other workplaces had created a private space for their Muslim employees to pray while they were at work.

While everyone was eating lunch, she found Mr. and Mrs. Medina in their office.

"Julia? What's up?" Mr. Medina spoke with his mouth full of lunch. Something green had attached itself to his gum.

"Well." She cleared her throat, pushed a bit of hair back under her uniform hat. "I would like—"

Mrs. Medina cut her off. "You have something there," she said to her husband, touching her own gum. "Do you want me to get it?" She did not wait for Tulio's answer. She pulled up his lip and wiped away the offending cilantro leaf. It was this kind of immediate attention that had guaranteed their business success; if they thought something needed to be done, they leapt into action.

Julia began again. "I would like to propose that Chimbley's Chocolates make a space for daily prayer in the same way as it has made a space for daily reading. For Osman."

The next morning, they assembled their employees to make an announcement. "Mr. Medina and I, at Julia's suggestion, have transformed our old office into a new space for prayer or meditation. All employees are invited to use it. We feel certain that this arrangement will allow you all to make the most of your workday, and will not stand in the way of our productivity."

The employees were then invited to poke their heads into the Prayer/Meditation Room. Inside they saw small gestures that hinted at a variety of faiths—a prayer mat, an altar with fruit and incense, some white flowers, a crucifix, a Star of David, a velvet cushion. And a CD player, with a small stack of CDs beside it, so that if someone wanted to fill the room with music, they could. The employees took it all in—the office that had once been the nerve center of the business—a ringing telephone, stacks of paper, file upon file—was now an oasis of tranquility. It was difficult to believe that a small business was going to all this trouble to be good to its employees.

Mr. Medina added, "We're not at the point when we can give you the kind of paid vacations we'd like to offer, but at least we can make a little part of every workday less stressful."

For Osman, it wasn't the prayer mat that caught his attention; it was the CD player with the stack of CDs beside it. When he saw that he had free access to an electrical device that could fill the small room with music, a weight lifted off his chest and his breath came more easily.

A week before Christmas, with her co-workers gathered beside her, Julia presented Osman with their gift. "We want you to know that the Christmas tree is not Christian,

Osman. It is two things—a celebration of winter and a reminder that green leaves will return in the spring. The tree with lights is for everyone because everyone in the world shares the same sun."

As he accepted the gift from her, his eyes were a window to his gratitude. He could tell that she had thought carefully about her words, selecting them in the hope that nothing she said would prompt his bad memories to return.

When he arrived home with the little fir, he was questioned. *Osman! What are you doing? Are you converting? Leaving your faith?*

"No, brothers. I just want to celebrate everything. This Tree of Light reminds me that the sun shines even in the darkest months."

His roommates did not argue with him, but they treated him like his blood brothers had—like he was unusual. And he was: while they cut meat in the halal butchers, he packed dainty chocolates; while they wore aprons smeared with animal blood, he wore a uniform smeared with chocolate. At some point, each roommate had wondered privately what type of work this was for a man? But he had seemed happy, and they did not question his happiness, especially after all the grief they were sure, like themselves, he had suffered.

When Osman placed the little fir on the table by the window, his roommates looked at it with curiosity, but never came close enough to brush against its needles. Still, the lighted tree gave them something tender to look at, and so it was difficult to remain detached from its warmth.

Shortly before Christmas, Mr. and Mrs. Medina organized all Chimbley's Chocolates employees—the Roasting Room, the Kitchen, the Wet Room—for an evening of door-to-door caroling. (They voted to donate any money they collected to the Refugee Relocation Center.)

When the evening was first discussed, Osman had asked, "What is caroling?"

"Singing," said one co-worker.

"A carol is a religious song about Christmas. But these days it is also nonreligious songs too," said another.

"If you come with us, Osman, we will not sing religious songs, only happy songs about this time of year. There are plenty—White Christmas, Frosty the Snowman, I Wish It Could be Christmas Everyday, Santa Claus Is Coming to Town, Rocking Around the Christmas Tree . . . The list is endless. Come with us," pleaded Julia.

On Carol Night, he wrapped himself in layers and wore two pairs of socks inside his boots. The Chimbley's employees congregated outside the Mogadishu Business Center, across the street from his apartment. All thirty-two had turned up. As he joined the carolers, he could see his roommates looking down at him, their foreheads pressed against the livingroom window. The lights from the small tree highlighted their faces. He waved. They waved back.

"Who's that?" asked Julia.

"My roommates."

"This is where you live?"

"Yes. That is my window."

"Let's go!"

The Chimbley Chocolate's carolers crossed the street and rang the top bell. By the time the three Bantu men came down the stairs, the group was already mid-song:

You will get a sentimental feeling
When you hear
Voices singing let's be jolly
Deck the halls with boughs of holly

Osman stood at the back, his smile wider than everyone else's. Julia sang beside him, the beauty mark above her lip now a smudge of chocolate. Her voice was strong and loud, and it lifted his voice, which helped him to reach the notes that would have been a struggle without her throaty sound. He sang the English words with an ease that was not present when he tried to speak this new language.

His roommates had not seen this side to him. They had not heard him sing once—no childhood songs, no grownup songs. No singing at all.

The thirty-two singing mouths before them coaxed the Bantu men out of their doorway and into the street. As the song enveloped them, their bodies relaxed. This was the first time since their arrival in Maine that they had stood outside at night without wondering if someone would jump out of hiding to attack them.

When the first song ended, the carolers began another:

When the snowman brings the snow
Well, he just might like to know
He's put a great big smile
On somebody's face

The night was cold enough for the snow to stick, to pile up into a foundation—something clean and soft on which they could build a future.

Notes

"The Evolution of Beauty" references Richard Prum's book by the same name.

"God is Merciful" was inspired by the sentence, "The mistake she made was going back for her cow," as reported on *BBC World News* radio, May 2011.

"Osman's Window" includes excerpts from the 22 July 2016 article in *Al Jazeera*, "Black man 'shot by police' while helping patient."

Acknowledgements

Thank you to the editors of the following journals where some of these stories were previously published in slightly or vastly different versions of themselves: *The Denver Quarterly*, *Natural Bridge*, *GenPop Magazine*, and *Duende*.

Toda to Lauren Sanders. *Mahalo* to Rahna Reiko Rizzuto. *Do jeh, daw-dyeh* to Aimee Liu. And *takk* to John McManus. These little sentences cannot adequately express my appreciation for your generous hearts and your time.

And ευχαριστώ to Christian Peet. Χωρίς εσένα δεν θα υπήρχε αυτό το βιβλίο.

Ten percent of the profit of sales of this book will be donated to the Vermont Refugee Resettlement Center (VRRP). The VRRP is the Vermont office of the U.S. Committee for Refugees & Immigrants and the only refugee resettlement agency in Vermont. Over the past 30 years, VRRP has developed an effective, efficient resettlement program. The Department of State recognizes VRRP as one of the best resettlement agencies in the country. With the help of the Vermont community, VRRP continues to provide refugees with vital services and a warm Vermont welcome.

About the Author

Elena Georgiou is the author of two collections of poetry, *Rhapsody of the Naked Immigrants* (Harbor Mountain Press), and *mercy mercy me* (University of Wisconsin), which won a Lambda Literary Award for poetry and was a finalist for the Publishing Triangle Award. She is also co-editor (with Michael Lassell) of the poetry anthology, *The World In Us* (St. Martin's Press).

Georgiou has won an Astraea Emerging Writers Award, a New York Foundation of the Arts Fellowship, and was a fellow at the Virginia Center for the Creative Arts. Her work appears in journals such as *BOMB*, *Cream City Review*, *Denver Quarterly*, *Duende*, *Gargoyle*, *Lumina*, *Natural Bridge*, and *Spoon River Review*. She is an editor at Tarpaulin Sky Press and the Director of the MFA in Creative Writing program at Goddard College.

Georgiou is originally from London, England, where she spent the first twenty-seven years of her life. Since then, she has lived in the US—first in New York, now in Vermont.

CPSIA information can be obtained
at www.ICGtesting.com
Printed in the USA
LVHW02s1921260218
567907LV00003B/286/P